The Home Child

A Supernatural Novel

Lynn L. Clark

The Plaid Raccoon Press
2014

The Home Child is a work of fiction. All names, characters, institutions, places and events portrayed in this novel are either the product of the author's imagination or are used fictitiously. Any resemblance to actual persons, living or dead, events or locales is entirely coincidental.

Book design: Michael J. McCann

Front cover design: Michael J. McCann
Front cover photographic image: public domain

Back cover design: Michael J. McCann
Back cover image: Sascha Burkard/Getty Images. Used under license.

In memory of my mother, Muriel Annie Clark, whose heart always went out to the disadvantaged.

1

Jake thought he was being watched.

For about the fifth time, he glanced at the darkened window, only to see his own reflection and the tree branches driven by the wind across the windowpanes. He turned back to the computer screen and the article he was composing.

As a freelance journalist, he had purchased this 100-acre farm for some privacy and a quiet space to write. Was there such a thing as too much seclusion? Tomorrow he would try to find some curtains for the windows because they were creeping him out. The last time he glanced up, he was almost certain he could see blurred movement in the periphery.

Great! Maybe I should start writing horror novels. A poor man's Stephen King.

Better to shut it down for tonight and start again in the morning after a cup of coffee.

Jake Hall had spotted the newspaper ad for the property about eight months ago. It was described as a fixer-upper, which he knew was realtor-speak for a falling-downer, but he decided to have a look anyway. What he encountered on his first visit—despite the forced optimism of the real estate agent—was a huge house with doors and windows that buckled and let in cold air, a leaking roof (he'd deliberately chosen a rainy day to view the house), antiquated wiring and plumbing, and a growing mouse population. What appealed to him was the quiet of the property with its massive trees and a small stream running behind it.

The real estate agent had talked about the acreage and how he could sell the hay to nearby farmers. She also mentioned that he could fix up the barn and rent out the stalls to horse enthusiasts. All of this seemed a bit overwhelming for someone who had spent almost his entire adult life living in a high-rise apartment building, but he was willing to give rural living a try, if only to escape from the constant traffic congestion and noise of the city. He knew that in spite of all the needed repairs, the property was selling at a fraction of its worth in a slumping real estate market.

Once he decided to buy the property, he managed to wrangle a loan with his bank, although the bank manager acquiesced only because he thought Jake would invest some money and flip the property to some other disenchanted city dweller.

But Jake had stuck with it. He had rented a U-haul and had moved his belongings into the house in mid-October of the previous year in a single trip from Ottawa. A friend—highly skeptical of his new living arrangements—had accompanied him to help with the move. Not being a handyman, Jake had enlisted local help to repair the roof before the first snowfall, put in new bathroom plumbing and fixtures, upgrade the wiring, and replace the doors and windows. Jake himself had spent several weeks removing the ancient, stained oilcloth from the floors and varnishing the hardwood underneath. He was currently furnishing its many rooms one at a time with finds from flea markets, yard sales, and a local antique shop, and the house was actually starting to look lived-in.

He had given some of the rooms only a cursory look and had yet to explore the attic, fearing that the mice up there might have built a lair equivalent to the alien queen's in that Sigourney Weaver movie.

❧ ❧ ❧

2

It was morning. Jake was feeling somewhat groggy from a restless night on a lumpy mattress that he had yet to replace. It was probably a three-coffee minimum this morning. He fired up his computer and grimaced at what he had written last evening. Not exactly inspired writing, even for an economist. His background in economics and journalism allowed him to make a modest income as a freelancer. Currently, he was writing a monthly series called "The Armchair Economist" for a business journal, sort of a dummy's guide to the economy that was the brain-child of a publisher trying to attract a wider readership. This particular segment was on maximizing investments in the stock market.

He looked at what he had written so far: "Given

the current economic uncertainty..." This was the business journal equivalent of Bulwer-Lytton's "It was a dark and stormy night." Time for another coffee.

After two more coffees, the article began to flow, and when he next looked at the time in the right-hand corner of the computer screen, he realized it was almost 3 PM. He had missed lunch, but one of the advantages of living alone was that he could eat when he felt like it. He went to the kitchen and prepared one of his all-time favourites: a toasted bologna sandwich slathered with mayonnaise. As he sat at the kitchen table and glanced out the window, he saw that several large branches had fallen across the lawn from last night's storm. He made a mental note to clear them after he'd finished eating.

The sky looked like rain was threatening, so Jake fished in the closet under the front staircase where he thought he had last deposited his raincoat and gum rubber boots. As he grabbed for his raincoat, it fell to the floor and settled on a pair of boots, probably belonging to a child. He had not seen them before.

Must have been left here by a family member of the Warrens, the previous owners.

It sounded plausible, but that did not explain the wet mud still clinging to the soles.

Once outside, Jake gathered the fallen branches in his wheelbarrow and deposited them by the woodpile in case some of them could be salvaged for kindling. It was late April with a bite in the air, and although he'd had a new oil furnace installed, he still liked to use the old wood stove in his kitchen. It seemed to dispel the chill of the house.

The ground was muddy, and on impulse he walked around to the corner of the house where his study was located. Near the windows were unmistakable footprints and the imprint of a small, muddy hand on one of the windowsills.

His house was obviously too far out in the country to attract a peeping Tom, so he could not explain what he was seeing. The prints looked like those of a child, but there were several fields separating him from his nearest neighbour and, in any event, the McFarlanes had no children living at home that he knew of.

Jake felt a chill down his spine. If his mother were still alive, she would say that someone had just walked over his grave.

When he returned to the house, he decided to spend a few minutes pinning up sheets to cover the study windows. He had installed blinds on most of the other windows in the rooms he was using, but for some reason had decided to leave the windows bare in this room. As he drove the push pins into the wooden frame, he averted his eyes from the muddy prints outside, although he could not rid himself of his feeling of discomfort. He would be going into town tomorrow and would buy some blinds to fit the windows, but the makeshift curtains would do for now.

He decided to forgo any additional work on his computer and instead moved to his living room, which contained his music system, leather couch and love seat, plasma television, and other furniture from his old apartment, plus a few antiques he had recently purchased. He had splurged on a satellite dish because there was no cable service this far out in the country, but he probably could have spared himself the expense: as usual, there was nothing on worth watching. After much channel surfing, it came down to a choice between *Dogs with Jobs* and the home decorating channel. He opted for the former.

Jake pulled his exercise mat and treadmill from the corner of his living room into the middle of the room, lowered the volume on the television, and began his workout, while glancing periodically at the television screen. A beagle diligently sniffed away, greatly embarrassing a traveller who had failed to declare to Customs the homemade sausage tucked away in his luggage.

Jake supposed that he could get a dog now that he was out of the high-rise. He made a mental note to check the nearby animal shelter for possible candidates. His preference was a larger dog, probably a Golden Retriever because of their beauty and temperament. Who knows? He might have better luck with a dog as a companion. His last relationship had gone nowhere. When what's-her-name had left him shortly before he moved here, she'd told him he was "a nice guy," but that she was not ready to settle down with one partner. She had underscored this fact by sleeping with his ex-best friend.

After an hour of exercise, he switched off the television and went to the upstairs bathroom to shower. He found this evening routine—the reverse of his city jogging sessions in the early morning hours—seemed to clear his mind and help him sleep. As he soaped himself and shampooed his hair, he happened to glance at the water circling the drain. He thought the new plumbing had solved the problem with rusted pipes, but as he continued to watch, the water turned to a rust colour that shone like blood in the glare of the fluorescent bathroom lights.

For a moment, he felt nauseated—as if the blood were real.

The day's events had unnerved him, and sleep would not come. Jake re-read an old paperback Stephen Frey novel—he was between books, as well as girlfriends—and finally fell asleep with the light on around 12:30 AM.

He startled awake to a sound that was somewhere between the ringing of a telephone and the persistent buzzing of a doorbell. As he struggled to become fully awake, Jake realized it could be neither because he didn't possess a land line nor have a doorbell. He glanced at his cell phone on the nightstand to see if it was ringing. But the screen was blank and the phone was mute.

And that was it for sleep.

❧ ❧ ❧

3

Jake had a fairly flexible schedule. He was content to put in at least six hours a day writing and keeping up to date on the stock market and various new business trends. The remainder of his day was usually spent on the house, doing the painting and minor repairs of which he was capable. Now that spring had arrived, he would also put in some hours outside to prune the trees and clean the barn. The wraparound porch was settling into the ground and might need a new foundation, and he had added this to his mental to-do list for tasks requiring outside help.

Jake also liked to fix up old furniture that had

been abandoned by previous generations of owners. He had discovered a small, cluttered antique shop stuck in a dusty storefront off the main street. The owner's name was Gertie, and she was a lively seventy-something with a wicked sense of humour. Nothing in the store was organized or priced, but if you managed to unearth a treasure, Gertie would give you a fair price on it. Currently, Jake was stripping by hand and restoring an antique wash stand that he had unearthed at Gertie's beneath a massive pile of old *Reader's Digest* magazines.

Today was Tuesday, which was "town" day when he made the fifteen-minute drive into the nearby town to run errands and pick up groceries. He had settled on this day after much trial and error, discovering that the sales in the local flyers ended Wednesday or Thursday; that on weekends the local grocery stores were crowded with impatient shoppers; and that Monday wasn't a good day to shop because the merchants hadn't had time to restock shelves from the weekend. So Tuesday it was, and it was a trip that Jake looked forward to primarily because he used it as an excuse to sample the home-cooking at a local restaurant owned by Betty Gerritsen, visit the antique shop, and chew the rag with Betty and Gertie, who were fast becoming his only friends in the area.

This Tuesday as he walked into the restaurant, Betty called out to him. "I was waiting for you. I have a new sandwich I want you to try. Think you're up for it?" Betty liked to kid him about his lanky frame, saying he could barely cast a shadow unless she fattened him up. So far, she had been doing a good job: he had gained at least ten pounds in the seven months since moving here.

"I'm starved, Betty. I've been running errands all morning. Bring it on."

As she cleared a small wooden table for him and washed the surface, he noticed—not for the first time—that she was a lovely woman. She reminded him a great deal of his mother, who had retained her beautiful blue sparkling eyes until her death. He had read somewhere that the eyes were the only part of the face that didn't age outwardly. Betty was probably on the far side of sixty, but her face was unlined, except for the smile lines bracketing her mouth and the wrinkles near the corners of her eyes, showing that she was quick to smile and laugh. In a community that frequently regarded you as a stranger unless you had lived here all your life and your family went back at least four generations, Betty was an exception. She had been kind to him since the first time he'd stepped into her restaurant.

"So, Jake. How's your search for a new girlfriend?" Betty was an eternal optimist as far as relationships went, and as soon as she discovered that Jake was single and nearing forty, she had been trying without success to match him up with every available female member of her family under the age of sixty.

"Not so good, Betty. I'm thinking of getting a dog instead."

Betty screwed up her face and laughed. "Dogs are good, Jake, but maybe you should try to find some human companionship. It must get pretty lonely out there knocking around in that big old house."

"So far, I'm too busy to notice. I still haven't tackled the attic. 'I hate those meeses to pieces'," he said, using the line from an old Hanna-Barbera cartoon he had watched on YouTube.

"Hell, Jake, I think you should invest in some cats first, before you get a dog."

"Could be, Betty. Might help cut down on my rodent population. I don't like being outnumbered in my own house."

After trying the new sandwich, which consisted of caraway bread with alternating layers of thinly-sliced ham and turkey topped by a slice of Swiss cheese and blue cheese crumbles and served with Betty's home fries, Jake could barely move. Betty took advantage of a lull in customers and pulled up a chair to join him. "So what do you think?" she asked eagerly.

"Wonderful," Jake exclaimed, "but then I can't imagine you making anything that isn't delicious." He patted his stomach by way of approval. Then, remembering the footprints outside his windows, he asked her if she knew whether the McFarlanes, his neighbours, had had their grandchildren visiting them lately.

"What makes you ask that?" Betty said, a bit sharply.

Not wanting to get into the details, Jake said he thought he had heard a child playing in the field near his property.

"You wouldn't know," Betty said, "being new to the area. Their first-born, Seth, died the crib death, and their two younger boys were drowned in the creek that runs back of your property. The McFarlanes don't have any children or grandchildren."

❦ ❦ ❦

4

The rest of the week was fairly routine as Jake finished his article and sent it via e-mail to his editor at the business journal. Aside from hearing what he thought were footsteps overhead in the attic, which he attributed to the mice and whatever else was up there, he had encountered no further episodes.

Betty's husband "Fred" was coming this weekend to have a look at the barn and see if it could be used in its present condition. This wasn't his actual name—which Jake had forgotten—but he was called this because he was short and squat and had a large round face and a goofy smile like Fred Flintstone. Even Betty called him Fred. He was a jack-of-all-trades: a plumber by profession, but also capable of wiring, building whatever needed building, and fixing up just about any kind of machine or vehicle. Jake knew he was extremely lucky to know someone this capable in all the skills he lacked, and Fred was very grateful for the work because he hadn't had a lot of paying jobs lately.

Jake heard the pickup round the corner and saw it turn into his driveway. Like most trucks in the country, it was dusty and pockmarked from the gravel roads. To his surprise, Betty was with Fred, grinning away and waving hello.

"I decided to come see what you've been up to here, and maybe lend you a hand in the attic while Fred's looking at the barn," she said as she closed the passenger door of the truck. "Seeing how fond you are of mice, I thought maybe you could use some company up there."

Jake could feel his face colouring. He had often poked fun at himself by recounting to Betty his close encounters with snakes, skunks (a near-miss for being sprayed), and raccoons. But Betty recognized beneath his humour that Jake hadn't quite adapted to the realities of country living, including mice seeking shelter in his house from the cold. She was obviously trying to help him out, for which he was very grateful.

"Let's go for it, Betty. Maybe there are some nice antiques up there that will make it worth our while."

As Fred left for the barn, he and Betty climbed the second stairway that led to the attic. "My grandparents had an old farmhouse like this," she reminisced. "The rooms just went on and on. I was only in the attic once with my grandfather, but it was neat and orderly like the rest of the house. Grandma wouldn't stand for cobwebs anywhere on the property."

"I guess she wouldn't like this place much," Jake replied. "Even the cobwebs have cobwebs," he said, raising his eyebrows in an imitation of Groucho Marx. Betty shook her head and laughed.

As he pulled up the latch on the door, he noticed the dust on the floor had recently been disturbed and, once again, he thought he could see small footprints. But Betty didn't seem to take notice as they moved into the attic.

There were three pull-chain lights that he turned on to dispel the afternoon gloom. Aside from several cardboard boxes in the corner that had obviously been chewed by mice, the room was empty except for three items in one corner. There was a small wooden trunk with worn leather fastenings, a child's bed with an iron headboard, and a battered child's desk with attached seat that looked as if it had been salvaged from an old school house.

"Let's take the boxes downstairs and see if there are any nests inside. You should probably grab that trunk as well and air it out," Betty said.

He and Betty carried the boxes and trunk downstairs and outside to the porch. Together, they emptied the contents and then folded the boxes and placed them in his wooden garbage bin. Most of the contents had been chewed and would have to be discarded, but he would sort through them later once the smell had aired out a bit.

As he went into the kitchen to wash his hands and get Betty a drink of water, he heard a shrill buzz. Seeing his startled look, Betty pointed to a plastic box on the front kitchen wall he had mistakenly thought was the cover of an old doorbell that had since been removed.

"That's the intercom system for the barn. The Warrens wired it in so they could communicate between the barn and house. I was visiting Lorraine Warren one day and saw her use it. Fred must be checking to see if it still works." She depressed the answer button and began talking to Fred.

But Jake wasn't really listening to her any more. He was thinking that this was the sound he had heard earlier this week in the middle of the night.

⊰ ⊰ ⊰

5

Fred advised Jake that the barn was in fairly decent shape, having been used by the Warrens for their animals. In fact, Fred explained, it was probably in better shape than the house because the former owners had tried to make a go of being self-sufficient, raising their own dairy cattle, pigs, and chickens, and bartering the hay in the fields for beef from the McFarlanes. They had also cleared large plots of land for gardening in back of the house.

Jake knew there were a number of riding schools in the region catering primarily to teenage girls who competed in local shows and equestrian events. He thought he would follow up on the suggestion of the real estate agent to rent out the stalls in the barn. He didn't know the first thing about raising farm animals, but he also didn't want the space to go to waste.

"I've made a list of materials I'll need so I can call you with some figures and maybe start next week if you want," Fred said.

Jake suddenly remembered the sagging porch. "Can you have a quick look at the porch while you're here, Fred? The foundation's really crumbling. I don't know if the porch can be propped up or if the whole thing needs tearing down and replacing."

Fred made the rounds of the porch and started ,jotting some calculations in his small notebook. He told Jake that he thought he could put in new posts supported by cement deck blocks. He would replace the stairs and railing because they were starting to rot.

After Fred and Betty left, Jake began looking at the contents he had removed from the cardboard boxes in the attic. The newspapers were yellowed with age, and many of the pages were stuck together from the moisture in the attic, but he decided he'd put them aside anyway.

At the bottom of the pile, he came across a velvet photograph album, which was faded and almost indistinct in colour. He undid the clasp on the album and opened it to an array of photographs of unsmiling men and women dressed in Victorian-era clothing and looking very uncomfortable. There were some older tintypes, as well as cabinet cards, whose format he recognized from having viewed several of them in Gertie's shop.

Tucked inside the album was a single photograph of a young boy, probably in his early teens. This photograph was different. It had not been carefully staged as had the others, and the child was wearing clothes that were obviously hand-me-downs because they were too big for him. He was standing in front of a dilapidated barn—probably long-since torn down. It was a clumsy attempt at photography: the picture had been overexposed. But Jake was drawn to the boy's eyes. He thought they were the saddest eyes he had even seen.

Jake did not sleep well that night. He dreamed of the boy in the photograph and near dawn he thought he saw someone standing beside his bed.

When he awoke, he found a very old edition of *Pilgrim's Progress* on his nightstand.

❦ ❦ ❦

6

The following Tuesday, Jake loaded the small trunk from the attic, which he had found to be empty, and the old photo album into his car. He had received a call from Gertie saying that she had some ladder-back chairs he might be interested in, so he decided to show her these items to get an idea of their age and provenance.

Gertie greeted him with enthusiasm as he entered the store and led him to a corner where several chairs had been placed together. "I got these at an estate auction on the weekend. They went cheap because the caning on the seats needs replacing."

Jake didn't know anything about re-caning the

seats, but he figured he could get some old pieces of leather to cover them for now. "How much, Gertie?"

"You can have the lot of them for a hundred dollars. They're old—probably turn of the last century—but I don't like to ask more 'cause of the seats. If they were in good shape, the chairs would be worth at least a hundred a piece."

"That's a bargain for six of them. I'll take them, Gertie. You got a minute to look at a couple of things I brought with me?"

Gertie laughed. "You going to start selling me stuff now?"

"No, it's just some things I found in the attic. I was curious about their age and who they belonged to. I thought you might know more about who owned the farm before the Warrens."

"Seeing as I'm older than God," she joked good-naturedly. "Go get them and I'll have a look."

Jake carried the trunk and photo album into the store. As soon as Gertie saw the trunk, she said, "That belonged to a home child, that much I know. The trunks were all made the same depending on the home they came from."

Jake said apologetically, "Sorry, I don't know much about the home children, other than the fact they came from Britain."

"I had a relative who was a home child, so I've done a fair amount of research. She was an aunt by marriage. The world was an emptier place when she died, let me tell you. She was one of the kindest and gentlest people I've ever known.

"Anyway, from what I know of the home children, they mostly came through the port of Halifax and then went inland by train. Most of them came to Ontario. There were homes in Peterborough and Belleville and Brockville that processed the kids, and then they went on to new 'homes' if you can call them that. They were farm labourers and domestic servants. Aunt Joan was one of the lucky ones. She was sent to a loving home in Canada. A lot of them ended up having pretty hard lives.

"They had a standard allotment of clothing, depending on whether it was a boy or girl, and some writing material although most of them were never allowed to write home. A lot of them never even knew their families. Did you find anything in the trunk?"

Jake shook his head and then asked Gertie if she knew of any farms in this area who had taken in home children. He showed her the old photo album and the picture of the boy.

As Gertie fingered the worn velvet on the cover, she said, "This was a beautiful album at one time. It probably dates from the 1880s because it has cabinet cards as well as the old tintypes.

"It's obvious that this picture of the boy doesn't fit. It was probably taken by an amateur photographer at a later date. It *could* be a home child. The time frame would be right and you've got the trunk as well.

"If you really want to do the legwork, you can talk to my niece at the library. She used to work for the federal government, and I think she was handling some project related to the home children. Her name is Jenny Campbell. If you want, I can call Jenny and see what her schedule is."

Jake nodded and said he would like to meet with her niece. After loading the chairs in his car, he thanked Gertie and prepared to leave. He still had to stop at Betty's restaurant and then buy groceries. But he suddenly thought of something and turned back at the door. "You mentioned the writing material. Did they put any books in the trunk that you know of, Gertie?"

"Yes. It was mostly church organizations who shipped these kids out. There was usually a Bible inside the trunk. I remember one group from Scotland put in a copy of *Pilgrim's Progress*. Stuck in my mind because I read the Classics Illustrated version when I was a kid. Scared the bejesus out of me."

❧ ❧ ❧

7

Gertie called him on his cell phone around 7 PM and told him her niece would be working tomorrow and Thursday if he wanted to stop by the library. She suggested that he take a photo of the trunk to show Jenny, as well as the picture of the young boy.

"Oh, by the way, make sure you get there before noon. Her boss, Jean-Michel Cormier, always checks in with her then, just in time to disrupt her lunch. He's a pompous ass, and he'd be likely to stick his nose in just to show you how important he is."

"I'll be sure to go early, Gertie. Thanks for the heads-up."

He was about to start working on another article

when he heard a vehicle in his yard. He looked out and saw Betty stepping down from her truck. He met her at the door.

She said hello, and Jake noticed that she looked a bit sheepish. "Remember when we were up in the attic, you mentioned that you were thinking over my suggestion about getting some cats. I hope it's not too forward of me, but I asked around. I found out that Vera Miller has to give up her two cats because she's going into a nursing home. She's very anxious to find a good home for them. They're both females, and usually they're better mousers. I thought you might be interested in taking them."

Jake smiled. "Well, I have been thinking about it. Maybe I should start off with the cats like you suggested. Hopefully, they'll be able to get along with a dog if I get one later. So maybe I can go see Mrs. Miller tomorrow."

"No need to, Jake." She reddened slightly. "I have them in the truck for you. I figured you'd be agreeable. Mrs. Miller sent their cages and some food and kitty litter. We just need to round up some bowls."

Jake helped her bring the two cages into the house. At first, the cats were wary and stayed inside their cages, but then one ventured out and the other followed. They both began sniffing around. He found some deep bowls and scooped out some cat food for them, and filled a dish with water while Betty poured kitty litter into the litter box she had brought with her. "You can sprinkle baking soda on the bottom to cut down on the odour."

They were beautiful cats. One was a calico, with an orange and black nose and black legs. Her name was, appropriately, Callie. The other was a long-haired black cat with piercing green eyes whose name was Licorice.

"Hope you're not superstitious about black cats," Betty said with a laugh. "I brought their vet records as well. They're both spayed and their shots are up to date. Vera got them at the same time from the animal shelter so they get along very well. They're both about five years old, which isn't that old in cat years. Some of them live to be twenty or older."

"Betty, just out of curiosity, did you have a Plan B if I said no?" Jake asked.

"Not really," Betty said, winking at him as she waved good-bye and closed the door to his house.

As she left, Jake thought: *I'm lucky she wasn't this forward with the match-making. Otherwise, she would have shown up at my door with one of her single relatives in tow.*

He spent the rest of the evening letting the cats roam around and sniff him before he bent down to pat them. They were both very affectionate and before long were rubbing against his legs and purring. He fixed up a couple of baskets with old bedding and placed them in the corner of his bedroom for them.

When he awoke during the night, he discovered the two of them sleeping soundly beside him on the bed.

≈ ≈ ≈

8

Jake started into town around 9 AM the next morning. He had taken a photo of the trunk, and also brought along the picture of the child and the copy of *Pilgrim's Progress* from his nightstand.

As he entered the library, a woman, who looked to be in her mid- to late-thirties, glanced up at him from her computer. She had pale blond hair, a shade lighter than Jake's. Her hair was tied back and fixed with some type of enamel barrette, he noticed. Her hair style and wire frame glasses accentuated the sharpness of her features.

She smiled and stood up to shake his hand. She was probably about 5' 10", Jake guessed, because she was only a couple of inches shorter than his 6-foot frame. She was thin and was dressed conservatively in black pants and a tailored white blouse, almost like a uniform. "You must be Jake Hall," she said. "Aunt Gertrude said you planned to stop by. I'm Jenny Campbell."

"I've been calling her Gertie. I hope that's not too familiar," he said as he shook her hand.

"No, that's what everyone else calls her. I just got used to calling her Aunt Gertrude when I was a little girl, and the habit stuck. She's my mom's older sister."

Jenny pulled out a chair and invited Jake to sit down beside her. She pointed to the book in his hands and asked if she might look at it. He also gave her the photo of the trunk he had taken with his cell phone and then downloaded and printed on his computer.

"How much do you know about the home children?" she asked him.

"Not a lot. Your aunt gave me a bit of background yesterday. She said she had a relative who was a home child."

"Yes. That was my great-aunt Joan. A wonderful lady.

"I was working for the federal government when the year of the home child was announced for 2010. I did a lot of research in preparation for the announcement so I looked at my old notes again yesterday when I heard that you'd be dropping by."

"To give you a quick overview, there were more than one hundred thousand children sent from the United Kingdom. The migrations began in the late 1860s and continued up until the start of World War II, although there were later migrations until 1948. About seventy per cent of the children came to Ontario.

"It was intended to be a rescue mission, believe it or not. If you've ever read Charles Dickens, you'll remember that the conditions in the city were pretty awful. There was a huge displacement of people from the country to work in the factories, children laboured for hours in unsafe conditions, and a lot of them just roamed the streets. The migration was supposed to give children like this a new start. That was the *intention*, anyway."

"What went wrong?" Jake asked.

"For one thing, it was understood that the children were to work in Canada as farm help and domestic servants until they were eighteen. Some of the children ended up with good families who adopted them, but a lot of them were exploited as cheap labour. They received virtually no education, and many of the farmers used them as substitute labour for their own children, who were then sent on to school while the home children worked the farm.

"The children were also supposed to be orphans, but we know now that only about two per cent of them actually were. Siblings got separated from each other, and some children temporarily placed in homes in the United Kingdom were there simply because their families had fallen on hard times. A lot of these children thought they had been abandoned by their families and didn't know what they had done wrong. Their 'crime' was being born poor.

"I'm sorry, I hope this doesn't sound like a lecture," she said, suddenly self-conscious.

"Not at all. It's something I'd like to know more about," Jake said, encouraging her to go on.

"The main thing that went wrong is that there was very little follow-up on the children. There were some annual reports issued, but they tended to whitewash the picture. And the organizations that sent the children over were paternalistic, thinking they knew what was best for the 'waifs and strays,' as they were sometimes called. It was the same way of thinking that led to the horrors of the residential schools in Canada."

Jake nodded, having read about the abuse at these schools for aboriginal children.

"Anyway, from the photograph of the trunk and the copy of *Pilgrim's Progress*, which I assume you found inside, I think this might be from one of the Quarrier homes in Scotland. William Quarrier was a philanthropist who founded the Orphan Homes of Scotland, from which many of the children came, although the majority came from the Barnardo orphan homes in England. That's why, by the way, they were called *home* children."

Jake handed her the picture of the young boy. She looked at it sadly and turned it over to see if there was any date or indication who had taken the picture. He explained that he had found it loose in an album of stylized photos.

"There are still some elderly folks around here who might know whether he was a home child," Jenny said.

"Do you think it would be okay if I contacted them to see if they recognize the child from the photo?" Jake asked. "Your aunt's been very helpful, but she just remembers the Warrens and the Millers before them. I actually checked the land registry office this morning before I came here, but there was no record of ownership earlier than the Millers. The clerk said the records had probably been lost. He didn't seem too interested, one way or another."

Jenny shook her head and laughed. "So you had the pleasure of meeting our registry clerk, Bentley. His father got him the job when he was deputy mayor. He's a bit, um, 'different' is the kindest way to put it, I guess. He spends his time waiting for the Rapture, so I've heard, and was very disappointed when the last prediction didn't come true. He'd already sold his house and arranged for someone to take care of his dog. Very sad, actually, when you think of it.

"What Bentley should have explained to you

is that a lot of early records were damaged before they could be digitized because a water pipe burst in the basement of the town hall a few years ago. I expect the records you're looking for must have been damaged or destroyed.

"But to answer your question about talking to someone who might know the boy in the photo, if you'd like to meet with the town's unofficial historian and you're a patient man," she smiled at this, "you can talk to Lorne Ramsay. He's about ninety-five, but he's still smart as a whip. The old-timers say that if Lorne doesn't know about it, it never happened.

"The only problem is that he tends to be very long-winded, and he digresses a lot. His nickname is 'Rambling Ramsay'. But he's a sweet old guy, and you just have to wait him out. If you want, I can arrange a visit for you. I can even go with you if that would make you feel more comfortable because he knows me well."

"That would be great," Jake said. "How about on the weekend?"

"Sure. I'll call him and let you know when we can meet with him. Do you mind if I ask you something though?"

"Fire away."

"You seem preoccupied with identifying this child. Do you think he's a relative of yours or something?"

"No," Jake said, "let's just say that I have some

ghosts to lay to rest." He gave her his cell phone number, and she also asked for his e-mail address, saying she would send him some links to the main internet research sites for people looking for information on home children.

When he returned to his house, the cats were glad to see him, rubbing against his legs. He reached down to pat them. "You guys are going to have to work for your chow. I need you to chase some mice out of the house. C'mon."

He had left the door of the attic open to air it out and also, he hoped, to interest the cats in the still-strong odour of the mice. But as he climbed the staircase, he noticed the door was closed and latched. The air was very cold.

There's probably a draft, he thought.

However, he couldn't account for the fact that the door was latched. If it had blown to because he had forgotten to close a window, that wouldn't explain how it got locked again. He pushed back the bolt, and tugged on the door, but it wouldn't give.

Paint sticking, he thought.

Finally, after a few harder tugs, it opened and he called the cats upstairs. They came bounding up, all playful and curious, but when they reached the doorway, they arched their backs, hissed, and refused to go inside the room.

❦ ❦ ❦

9

Jenny called him later that evening to tell him it was a go for their meeting with Lorne Ramsay on Saturday morning. She offered to pick him up, but he said he would come into town to save her the drive. She gave him her address, and he agreed to pick her up at 10 AM on Saturday. Apparently at his age, Lorne was a morning person, and reserved his afternoons for naps and his evenings for poker or other entertainment with his friends.

When they arrived at the assisted living quarters that Lorne occupied, Jake was surprised as the door opened. The man who greeted them was much younger looking than he had expected. His eyes were bright and sharp behind his horn-rimmed glasses, and his handshake was firm. He wore canvas pants with suspenders and a starched white shirt, as if he had dressed especially for their visit.

After the introductions were made, Jenny explained the type of information they were seeking. Jake showed Lorne the photograph of the young boy. Lorne smiled as he fingered the borders of the photo. "Looks like this was taken with an old box camera. Mother had one herself. Liked to take pictures of us kids in our Sunday best." This remark was followed by a dissertation on the Ramsay family with their six children, including the status and present whereabouts of each family member. Jenny smiled at Jake and he nodded, understanding that he would need to be patient.

When Lorne finally stopped to take a breath, Jenny tactfully led him back to the subject of the photograph and asked him if he knew who had owned Jake's farm before the Millers.

Lorne paused for a moment, as if deep in thought, and said that his mother had been a seamstress and often bartered her work for eggs and other farm produce after the death of his father in a logging accident. This prompted another aside on the death of his father and the current abysmal state of the logging industry. Then, back on subject, Lorne explained that his mother had told him stories of the various people for whom she had worked.

He recalled one incident in particular when his mother returned home in tears. He would have been about six or seven years old, Lorne reckoned. His mother had been visiting a local farm when she happened to glance outside. She saw a young boy stumbling behind plough horses while the farmer swore at him. She could see the child cowering as if afraid that the farmer would beat him.

She had inquired about the child with the farmer's wife, a small, timid woman who seemed equally cowed by her husband and did not want to intervene in the child's treatment. My mother said the woman just sat there, twisting her handkerchief, which smelled of lily of the valley, in her lap. Funny how that detail stuck with me.

"This distressed my mother to no end," Lorne said, sadly shaking his head at the memory. "She was a kind soul. She thought the boy was suffering, but didn't know what to do to help him. She made some inquiries with the child welfare people, but they didn't take her seriously. It was common in those days for some people to work children like animals. No one thought twice about it."

"Do you remember the name of the family she was visiting at the time?" Jenny gently prodded.

"Yes," Lorne said. They were the Fitzgeralds. The father was Abraham, if my memory serves. He was a miserable old sod from everything I've heard. I can't remember the wife's name. Abby or Abigail or

Anthea... something like that.

"I do recall my mother saying that Mrs. Fitzgerald near lost her mind from grief when her only son drowned in the creek that backed onto their property. He fell through the ice when skating one winter, and no one was there to save him."

❈ ❈ ❈

10

It was almost 1 PM when Jake and Jenny finished their meeting with Lorne, and they decided to get a sandwich at the local pub. Jake felt vaguely guilty for not eating at Betty's restaurant, but at the same time he was relieved that he could eat a meal without Betty's surveillance of his female companionship.

Jenny seemed more animated and relaxed outside the library, and Jake began to realize just how much he was enjoying her company. She was genuinely pleased about the meeting with Lorne and thought they were on the right track.

"Now that I have a name," Jenny said, "I can search the online censuses to see if I can find

Abraham Fitzgerald. It was fairly common practice to have home children listed as members of the household when a census was taken. I'm used to working with the censuses. You just need to know the best way to use the search function. With any amount of luck, I can put a name to the boy in the photograph. If not, there are still other sources such as passenger manifests, although that would be an onerous search since we don't know exactly when the boy came to Canada. There's also the Quarriers Society in Brockville. William Quarrier eventually set up his own receiving home, Fairknowe, for the children who came through that city. It's still there, by the way. It's been made into an apartment building."

Jenny excused herself after they had finished eating and said she had some errands to run. Her apartment was over one of the local stores so she didn't need a ride back. She promised to call Jake when she'd had time to look at the censuses.

"Thanks again for setting up the meeting and coming with me," Jake said.

Jenny smiled and touched his hand lightly before she left. "Talk to you later," she said.

Jake realized he was very much looking forward to their next meeting.

❦ ❦ ❦

11

One of the main selling points of the property he now owned was the stream running behind the fields. Jake had arranged to come back a few days after touring the farmhouse so he could see the property when it wasn't raining. He and the real estate agent had spent about forty-five minutes walking the property line, and she had shown him the stream—she had referred to it as the creek—which was the dividing line between the Warrens' property and the farm belonging to the McFarlanes. The water looked so peaceful to him at the time. He wasn't interested in fishing but he thought it would be great to sit beside the creek on a summer's day, and could picture himself bringing out his laptop to work here.

Now, within the space of two weeks, he had learned that the water was responsible for three deaths: the two McFarlane children, according to Betty, and the Fitzgerald boy, according to Lorne Ramsay, had drowned in that creek. He wondered if he would ever have the same feelings toward it as he'd had that day when he walked the property line. He also wondered if the real estate agent had known the history of tragedy attached to the creek.

Jake spent most of that evening looking at the websites that Jenny had recommended, especially the site for child migrations from the Quarrier homes in Scotland. He shook his head as he read some of the testimonies from the children themselves. As Gertie and Jenny had explained to him, some of the children had been adopted into good homes, but many were badly mistreated.

He decided he had better do some work on his next Armchair Economist article because he had been neglecting his writing lately. This one focused on the relationship between inflation and interest rates, in layman's terms of course.

He was finding it hard to concentrate after his research on the home children. These were children born into poverty who had never had much of a chance in life. He thought of the principles of population control that the English philosopher and economist Thomas Robert Malthus had laid out and how they had influenced Darwin's theory of natural selection and "survival of the fittest."

Malthus had believed that poverty was a direct result of the working class having too many children. He thought that charity toward the poor was misguided because it would only perpetuate the problem.

Jake remembered from his studies that the Poor Laws enacted in Victorian England to establish the workhouses with their subsistence levels of food were largely based on Malthusian principles. He thought of Scrooge in the opening scene of *A Christmas Carol*, refusing to donate to charity and asking sarcastically if there were no more workhouses. It was chilling, when you thought of it, that Malthusian principles of population control were still being debated today in such works as Dan Brown's *Inferno*.

After an hour, he gave up on the article for the evening and went to do his nightly exercise routine in the living room. He was surprised to find that the television set was already on, but set to mute so that he had not heard it. It was on the History channel and as Jake turned on the sound, he discovered that it was a documentary on the history of displaced persons from the British Isles.

Wait for it, he thought.

As he watched, photographs of young children boarding ships for Canada and Australia appeared on the screen with the trailer: British Home Children.

From his research, he recognized the name of one ship, the *SS Manitoban*. The television narrator explained that the ship was one of several of the Allan Line that had docked in Glasgow to carry home children to Canada from the Quarrier homes in Scotland until the vessel was scrapped in 1899.

The bleak faces of the children bore testimony to the fact that they were leaving familiar ground for a country they didn't know and that they would probably never return.

❧ ❧ ❧

12

After spending a restless night, Jake managed to sleep in until 8:30 AM. He shaved and dressed and was just finishing his coffee when Fred's pickup pulled into his yard. Fred had already done work to replace missing boards in the barn, and this morning he was going to start working on the sagging porch.

"Hi, Jake," he said, as he stepped down from the pickup. He reached in the back for his tools and then spotted the box of baked goods that Betty had sent. "Betty sent you this stuff, Jake. I think she's adopted you."

Jake grinned. "She's sure succeeding in fattening me up."

"You've got a ways to go, I think," laughed Fred, rubbing his pot belly. "Give her a few years."

Fred put his tools and lumber by the front steps and then Jake helped him unload the heavy cement blocks that would be used to support the porch. "We'll try these," Fred said, "but if they don't work, you're probably better off replacing the whole porch."

The two men cleared debris from below the porch, and Fred started preparing the ground for the cement blocks and the new posts. After the posts had been replaced and eight of the concrete blocks were in place, he asked Jake to walk on the porch to test it.

"It feels less rickety," Jake said, stomping heavily on the porch boards to see how they bore his weight. "I think I'll go with the blocks for now, Fred. I can't really afford a brand new porch. With the new stairs, I think it'll be okay."

"Spoken like a true optimist," Fred laughed, repeating the old line about a pessimist being an optimist with experience.

He then set about removing and replacing the old stairs and railing. In all, it was a five-hour job with Jake helping as best he could. Jake would never be a handyman, but at least now that he had worked beside Fred on various other projects, he could tell the difference between a Robertson and a Phillips screwdriver.

Fred was finished by 2 PM, and Jake paid him

and waved goodbye after ensuring that Fred would convey his thanks to Betty for the home-cooking she had sent.

It was now early May. The trees were green once again, and the huge lilac bushes that framed his driveway were in bloom. The smell wafted over to Jake, and he inhaled deeply. At times like this, he was very happy he had purchased the farm, and he felt a sense of accomplishment for the repairs and restoration that had already been performed on the house. Tomorrow he would put an ad in the local weekly papers to rent out the horse stalls.

After a quick bologna sandwich for lunch, Jake decided to spend a few hours working on his article. He finished it around 4 PM and then spent another hour doing revisions and a spell check before he sent it off to his editor. He would follow up next month with an article on the role of the Bank of Canada in regulating interest rates.

Jake's income from his freelance work was fairly modest, but he had an annuity from an insurance policy paid out after his mother's death. As an only child, he had also inherited his parents' house in Kanata, and he rented it out for the monthly income. He had continued the Warrens' barter arrangement with his neighbour, Jeremy McFarlane, exchanging his hay for eggs and beef. Jeremy had also plowed and tilled his back gardens for him and helped him plant potatoes, cucumbers, squash, tomatoes, and pumpkins. If this year's crop was good, Jake would be growing a lot of his own food. So although he wouldn't be buying a cottage in the Muskokas any time soon or wintering in Arizona, he had enough to live on. And if he was able to rent out the barn stalls, that would give him a bit more spending money.

Jenny called later that evening, sounding excited. She explained that the early censuses were conducted every ten years. Using the 1911 census as a baseline, she had found an entry for Abraham Fitzgerald. Also listed as members of the household were Alma Fitzgerald—Lorne had been close with the name—and a son, Jonathan, their only child who, according to Lorne, had later drowned. Jenny had then compared the census information for 1921. There was another name listed with the Fitzgeralds: a fourteen-year-old boy named Robert Wilson. She was certain she had found the home child from the old photograph, and Jake agreed to meet her at the library in the morning to go over the documentation.

Well, Robert, I think part of the mystery is solved, and I have a name for you.

Jake slept well that night. When he awoke, the photograph of the young boy, which he had left downstairs next to his computer, was propped against the lamp on his bedside stand.

❧ ❧ ❧

13

Jake made preparations to drive into town the next morning. He would combine his visit to the library to see Jenny with his usual weekly shopping trip.

He made the fifteen-minute trek to town, and ran the main street gauntlet of unsupervised construction trucks and crews building new subdivisions to accommodate commuters from Ottawa who wanted the rural experience combined with the much higher salaries of Ottawa. There was also a detour while a municipal crew did road repair. Adding to the general traffic malaise was the fact that a former mayor had installed several roundabouts, which were universally despised, in close proximity to one another.

Jake wondered what this town would eventually look like. It seemed to keep expanding and creating more "affordable" townhouses, yet it still prided itself on being "small town Canada," as a sign on the local car dealership used to proudly proclaim, according to Gertie. Jake doubted if the town could have it both ways.

As he drove over the bridge to the library, he noted that there were two new For Rent signs that had cropped up since his last town visit. The new stores in the old town section, as it was commonly referred to, didn't have much in the way of longevity. It seemed that they were written up in the local paper only to close shortly thereafter. He had personally watched the demise of a couple of small stores, and Gertie had advised him that many other stores had closed: a dress shop that catered to young women, a craft store, a scarf and accessories shop, a decorating shop, and a bead store, among others. A number of higher-priced restaurants and cafes remained, along with a jewellery store, two used bookstores, and a few specialty shops. It seemed to Jake that the problem, aside from the constant construction and road closures, was the fact that the stores that had disappeared had largely catered to niche markets. Of course, the rents were probably high too. This was certainly a problem with the mall on Highway 43, which had once thrived but now resembled a ghost town with its empty store fronts.

With her usual sardonic humour, Gertie had once told Jake that it was easier to outfit a dog than a person in this town: there were three pet stores (as well as numerous groomers). But aside from the hated big-box stores, there was really nowhere to purchase basic clothing, shoes, and household supplies. Jake reasoned that the big-box stores were in fact giving the town a fighting chance to encourage townspeople to shop locally rather than go to Brockville or Ottawa, with additional benefits for the farmers' market, local grocery stores, and restaurants.

He turned into the library parking lot, which was nearly empty at this hour. Jenny was working on a display of children's books. She looked up and smiled when he entered the library.

"Come over here, Jake," she said, gesturing to a table where a number of documents were spread out. "I found some additional information on the computer."

Jake joined her at the table after thanking her again for her help. She showed him the 1921 census information, the death certificate for Jonathan Fitzgerald, who was only sixteen when he drowned, and the death certificates for Abraham and Alma Fitzgerald, who died about three years apart.

"I found out through the online home child

database that Robert Wilson came to Canada in 1917, but I'm still trying to locate a death certificate for him. Robert Wilson is such a common name that there are dozens to sort through. He can't possibly be still alive. He was fourteen in the 1921 census, so his birth year was 1907. I'll keep looking, though. I love a good puzzle."

"Could I buy you lunch as a small down payment on all this work?" Jake queried.

"I 'm brown-bagging it today," Jenny said, "but I'd love to take a rain check. I'll be in touch when I find out more."

"Okay, that's a deal. By the way, I'm heading out to your Aunt Gertrude's place to see if I can find some outdoor light fixtures," Jake said. He described the work Fred had done and how he wanted the fixtures for his porch.

"Send her my best wishes," Jenny replied, as Jake gave a final wave and left the library.

Jenny smiled to herself as she resumed her work on the children's book display.

Gertie was of course surprised to see Jake on a Monday rather than his usual Tuesday, but he explained that he had been visiting her niece at the library.

"She's been very helpful," Jake said, and went on to describe the trail so far, and how Jenny had identified the home child—and most probably the boy in the photograph—as Robert Wilson.

"I'm sure Jenny has enjoyed helping you, Jake. She's been going through a very bad stretch this past couple of years, and I expect she welcomes the diversion."

Jake looked quizzically at Gertie, who said in an embarrassed tone, "I'm probably speaking out of turn. Jenny's not one to share her problems, but if you get to know her, she'll no doubt confide in you." Quickly changing the subject, Gertie asked Jake if there was anything in particular he was looking for today.

After spending twenty minutes sorting through cardboard boxes in the back room, Jake came upon some old brass fixtures that he could polish and have Fred wire into the porch. As usual, Gertie was very reasonable with her price.

After saying goodbye to Gertie and asking her to put aside some books for him for his next visit, Jake decided to finish off his normal routine by stopping by to see Betty and then picking up a few groceries.

Betty was happy to see him, asking how the cats were doing as she seated him at his usual table.

"Great," he assured her. "They act like they own the place."

"That's great, Jake. Pretty soon they'll be solving all your mice problems."

Jake didn't bother mentioning that the cats were too afraid to go up into the attic. Instead, he changed the subject. "What's new on the menu, Betty, since my last visit?"

Have I got a treat for you, Jake. I'm glad you came a day early. Are you hungry?"

"Ravenous, Betty."

"This is my latest. I thought it would be popular with the yuppies from Ottawa. Not you, of course, Jake," she hastened to add. "You're different." She scurried off to the kitchen without further comment.

In about fifteen minutes, she returned with a plate of catfish with Cajun seasonings, sweet potato wedges with sea salt and rosemary, and a salad with lettuce, slivered almonds, black olives, and balsamic vinegar dressing, along with her freshly-baked cheddar biscuits.

After taking his last bite with Betty hovering over him, Jake proclaimed the meal to be another one of her great successes. She beamed in response and hurried back to the kitchen to fetch him a piece of her home-made fruit pie.

❦ ❦ ❦

14

On his way home from town, Jake thought of Gertie's remarks about Jenny. He had sensed an aura of sadness about her and hoped that she would soon feel comfortable enough with him to share her burden. He realized that he was fast becoming very fond of her.

As he pulled into his gravel driveway, he noticed the flag was up on his mailbox. He opened it up to find several advertisements—this must have been the tenth flyer he had received so far this year for water softeners and at least the fifth postcard and fridge magnet from a local dentist soliciting new patients. There was also a notice from Canada Post saying that his mailbox was in contravention of the Rural Mail Guidelines, namely that:

> *A resident's name or address information must be placed on the side of the box so it is clearly visible to the delivery agent as he or she approaches the mailbox.*

Jake shook his head at this. This was at least the third time he had run afoul of Canada Post. The last time was in winter when Jeremy McFarlane's snowplow had knocked his mailbox over. Before Jake had had time to put it in place again, the delivery person had dutifully stuck a copy of the guidelines in his front door, highlighting the part that said the client must provide an *upright* mail receptacle. He figured he was lucky to get mail at all these days, what with all the cutbacks at Canada Post.

Licorice and Callie were at the door to greet him, meowing plaintively to express their displeasure at his absence. He rubbed their heads and re-filled their food bowls.

He reached into his pocket for his cell phone to check his messages. Like most people of his generation, he relied heavily on his electronic devices, including his cellphone, laptop, and e-reader. However, he had drawn the line at investing in a tablet, which he thought would be too cumbersome. He kept his phone with him at all times: it was almost an extension of his body, so he was surprised to find that it was not in his right-hand jeans pocket where he normally kept it. Jake began to scour the kitchen looking for it and finally located it on top of his fridge. He had no earthly idea how it had ended up there.

He discovered that he had a message from his editor, Jarrod Hunt, telling him to call. When Jake called him, Jarrod answered on the first ring and asked him when his latest installment of the Armchair Economist series would be sent. They needed it to finish off the page proofs. Jake replied that he had sent it on the weekend.

"The only thing I got last week from you was an e-mail with some gibberish about a golden bridge," Jarrod said. "Do you have a pseudonym now, by the way? There was the name 'Robert' in the signature block. I figured you must have finally gone nuts out there in the boonies. Didn't you get my e-mail asking what the hell was up?"

"I'll send you the article right away," Jake said, distractedly, and hung up.

He went to his laptop and found the e-mail he had sent to Jarrod. He opened it up. Instead of his article, there was the following text:

> *Give us the power to make a*
> *Golden Bridge across the Atlantic.*

From his previous night's research, Jake

recognized the frequently-quoted statement of Annie MacPherson, one of the pioneers of the child migration project. It was the irony of the reference to a *golden* bridge, given the miserable outcome for many children, that made the phrase stick in his mind, as well as the fact that *the golden bridge* was also the name of the website devoted to Scottish child migration from the Quarrier homes. He also noted, with shaking hands, that his signature block had been changed, as Jarrod had pointed out on the phone.

Jake turned next to his inbox, but could find no e-mail from Jarrod. He accessed his most recent Armchair Economist article from his saved documents, prepared another e-mail to Jarrod with the article as an attachment, and sent it off immediately. Within a few minutes, he received Jarrod's reply stating that he had received the article and that it looked good and would probably require few edits. Jarrod finished his e-mail by suggesting good-naturedly that Jake move back to civilization before he went completely starkers.

Jake suddenly felt overwhelmed by everything that had been happening to him and began to question his judgment in buying this house. Taken individually, he could probably laugh off these various episodes, but this altered e-mail was the final straw. Worse yet, he didn't feel comfortable talking to anyone about these incidents: the feeling of being watched; the muddy boots and prints outside his window; the displaced book and photo; the television program; the footsteps overhead; the intercom from the barn; and now this.

He did what he had not done for a long time: he nursed a fifth of Jim Beam, feeling very sorry for himself.

Around 2 AM his car alarm, which he had not set since he moved from Ottawa, began to blare, but by that time he had fallen into an uneasy sleep on his living-room couch.

❧ ❧ ❧

15

Jake swallowed some aspirin to ease his headache the next morning and decided he was going to try to be pro-active in finding out just what the hell was going on in his house.

After painting his name and civic number on the mailbox to ensure continued mail delivery, he washed up and went to his computer. He was not only going to continue his research on the home children, but was also going to look up some information on ghosts.

Jake was amazed at the amount of online information available. Being a novice in all things supernatural, he spent several hours doing research, making notes, and becoming more and more fascinated as he continued. He learned, for example, that a haunting was considered to be a manifestation of residual spiritual energy. Sometimes the "ghost" did not even realize he was dead. He immediately thought of the movie *The Sixth Sense.*

He also noted the wide divide between the paranormal investigators, who for the most part seemed to take their investigations very seriously, and the skeptics, who regarded paranormal investigation as a pseudo-science. After what had happened since he'd moved into this house, Jake was willing to keep an open mind. After all, he figured that if most religions espoused the belief in an afterlife, it was not much of a stretch to believe that something remained behind of a person after death.

What struck him most in his readings, however, were the continual references to the signs of haunting, many of which he had already experienced: the noises, the cold spots, the feeling of being watched, the television turning on by itself—this was referred to as "mild psychokinetic phenomenon"—and the displacement of objects. He thought of the boy's photo and his misplaced cell phone. Even the appearance of hand- and footprints was documented, although much less frequent an occurrence.

Jake wasn't at the point of calling in a paranormal investigator, but he did like the suggestion on one of the internet sites of keeping a journal to record his experiences. This appealed to his innate sense of logic. It also seemed to be a pro-active approach: one that would make him feel less helpless.

The day passed without further incident as Jake continued his research and began his journal, trying to remember, as best he could, the date of each episode. He realized that the episodes had accelerated in frequency once he and Betty had discovered the trunk in the attic. His working hypothesis—provided there was no logical explanation for each of these episodes, and he could find none—was that the spirit of Robert Wilson still lingered in his former home. But there were still too many unanswered questions. When and how had he died? Was he an orphan or, like many of the home children, simply from a poor family without the means to support its children? What unfinished business did he have in this house? His tormentor, Abraham Fitzgerald, was already dead, so it was too late to exact revenge. Besides, Jake didn't sense any malevolence in this spirit, but simply a desire to communicate. It was much more likely that the spirit of Robert Wilson was trying to seek Jake's help in reuniting him with his family in Scotland.

Jake set up a new e-mail account devoted specifically to inquiries regarding Robert Wilson. He posted notices on various sites, advising that Robert had come to Canada in 1917 from the Quarrier homes in Scotland, and requesting information on

Robert, his parents, any known siblings, and the circumstances of his death in Canada. He asked anyone who thought he or she might be a descendant of Robert Wilson to contact him.

Jake looked up from his computer, listening to the sound of his neighbour's tractor in the distance. As part of their barter arrangement, Jake had agreed to allow Jeremy McFarlane to cultivate two of his large fields and plant corn, which Jeremy would sell at the local farmers' market.

It was an unusually hot day for mid-May so he decided to take Jeremy some ice water. As he approached the field, he saw that Jeremy was wiping his brow and taking a break. He waved when he saw Jake, and stepped down from his tractor.

"I figured you could use some water about now," Jake said. Jeremy nodded his thanks as he took a long swig from the water bottle Jake handed him.

"I'm glad you stopped by, Jake. I keep meaning to tell you that there's an old well in the corner of that field you asked me to plow: the one you planned to set up with jumps if you were able to rent out your barn stalls. The well's dry, but the boards covering it have rotted. Best to have them replaced. A horse could break its leg if it stepped into those rotten boards."

Jake thanked him and added the task to his mental to-do list. He would probably get Fred to do it. On a whim, Jake decided to ask Jeremy about the previous owners of his house. "I know you had a barter arrangement with the Warrens," Jake said. "Did you see them a lot... I mean were you friends with them?"

"They pretty much minded their own business," Jeremy said, and Jake sensed an implied rebuke in that statement as if he would be wise to do the same. Jeremy thanked him for the water, climbed back on his tractor, and started it before Jake could utter another word.

Feeling unsettled when he returned to his house because of Jeremy's abruptness, he decided to call Janet Wheeler at the local real estate office. She was the real estate agent who had sold him the property. She sounded a bit tentative when she answered the phone and found out who was calling, as if expecting Jake to complain about the house. He assured her that he had called simply to get some additional information about the previous owners because he was interested in the history of the house. "You mentioned when you sold me the house, Janet, that the Warrens were moving to Ottawa. Had they owned the house for a long time?"

Janet hesitated and then replied that the Warrens had lived there about eight years. "They were childless and didn't need the extra space," she said.

"I know this will sound a bit weird, Janet, but did they give any other reason for leaving?"

There was a long pause. "Like what?" Janet finally replied.

"Anything about the house itself?" Jake asked, as innocuously as possible, and then hastened to reassure her that he had no complaints, but was just curious.

There was another long pause. Finally, Janet said: "Some people like to talk about their homes as if they have a personality. 'This is a warm house' or 'this is a welcoming house'. You know what I mean, Jake?"

"Yes," Jake said. "What type of personality did they give to this house, Janet?"

Biting off her words, Janet said reluctantly: "It was very silly, really, but they thought the house was cursed."

⋇⋇ ⋇⋇ ⋇⋇

16

The next morning, Jake put the garbage out for the weekly collection. He was about to close the bin when he noticed the newspapers from the attic that he had put aside. They were smelling less musty so he gathered them up and took them inside the house.

The papers dated from 1917 and contained a mixture of war news and local events. There were a number of articles on home children sent to the local farms, but no mention of Robert Wilson or the Fitzgeralds.

He glanced at the classifieds and noted with amusement the price of livestock and farms. *We should be so lucky today.* However, when he turned to the birth and death announcements, he felt a cold chill run down his spine. The majority of the obituaries in this immediate area related to the deaths of children.

He thought of the previous owners of the house, the Warrens, and remembered they were childless. His neighbours, the McFarlanes, had lost one child to crib death and the others to drowning. And the Fitzgeralds had lost their only son to drowning.

Had this chain of deaths, in fact, begun with the Fitzgeralds? It seemed like superstition to think that the events were related, but he began to understand why the Warrens had believed the house was cursed.

Jake wanted more than anecdotal evidence. He went online to see if he could find some statistics on birth and death rates in the county. He discovered that between the mid-1920s and the present day, there was a higher than average death rate for children, many of whom had not lived beyond the age of eighteen.

He was struck with a sudden thought and sent a text to Jenny to ask if any of the Robert Wilsons she had thus far tracked down died in 1925 or earlier. The home child Robert Wilson would have been 18 years old at that time.

Jenny responded later that evening to tell him that she wasn't able to find a record of death for a

Robert Wilson that would fit into this time frame. *So much for my theory*, Jake thought.

❧ ❧ ❧

17

The rest of the week was uneventful, and on Saturday Jake made his monthly trip to Kanata to check with his tenant and arrange for any upkeep or repairs needed on the property. He asked Jenny if she would like to come along because he was planning to drive into Ottawa afterward. She accepted his invitation, saying it would be nice to be back in the "big city" again.

Jenny was waiting outside her apartment when he drove up. She was dressed casually in jeans and t-shirt, but the colourful scarf around her neck lent a touch of elegance to her outfit.

"What do you miss most about the city, Jenny?"

he asked, as they drove the busy highway to Ottawa.

"I miss the live theatre and the museums," she said, "and of course the canal and the Byward Market. But I definitely don't miss the construction and traffic congestion and the lack of affordable parking."

"How long did you work in Ottawa?" Jake asked. "You mentioned that you used to work for the federal government."

"Eight years. But, unfortunately, the cutbacks hit everything that was vaguely related to culture and arts and therefore wasn't generating revenue for the government. Our department had massive layoffs, like the CBC," she said, referring to the Canadian Broadcasting Corporation.

"Do you enjoy your work at the library at all?" Jake asked. "Your Aunt Gertrude implied that your boss is, um, a bit full of himself."

Jenny laughed. "Leave it to Aunt Gertrude not to mince words. And I'm sure she used more colourful language than that. But I don't really mind him. I just stroke his ego, convince him that all my ideas are his and therefore very brilliant, and figuratively pat him on the head and send him on his way. His time is too valuable to spend much of it at the library anyway. He has lots of committees to head and meetings to attend."

"Do you ever get tired of having to work for

someone who is obviously much less intelligent than you are?"

"I've never really thought of it that way. But I've had a lot of practice dealing with difficult people. After you've survived the management in the public service—although there are some very good managers—people like Jean-Michel are a piece of cake to deal with. My last manager before I left the public service terrified me. He was abusive to his employees and had a hair-trigger temper. I finally got fed up with his bullying one day and spoke my mind. Unfortunately, I was wound up and used the BS word. He turned beet red and looked like he was having a fit of apoplexy, and then threatened to charge me with insubordination. Like we were in the army or something. It's a good thing I didn't use the F-word. He probably would have had me arrested."

Jake laughed. "I can't imagine you using that type of language," he said.

"That's because you haven't seen me when I'm really angry," Jenny said, blushing.

Jake laughed. " I think I 'd enjoy seeing that."

When they reached Kanata, Jake asked if she would prefer to wait at the Tim Hortons while he visited his tenant so she wouldn't be bored, but she said she would enjoy seeing where he grew up.

Everything seemed okay at the house although he noticed that the lawn needed cutting and made a mental note to have this looked after. Bill Avery, his tenant, had no complaints. There had been an earlier problem with a leaky faucet, but Jake had arranged for a plumber to fix it. Bill worked at a local IT shop, was generally laid-back, and all in all was a very good tenant, especially after some of the rental horror stories Jake had heard.

"It looks like a lovely place," Jenny said, as Jake climbed back into the car. "I like the arbours and the climbing roses," she said. "It must have been a peaceful place growing up."

Jake nodded. "I used to think that nothing could ever touch this place—like it had its own bell jar. I guess every kid likes to think that about the place he calls home.

"Unfortunately, reality caught up with it. My dad died of prostate cancer about ten years ago, and my mom died of a heart attack two years later. It never felt the same in that house after their deaths. I wasn't ready to sell it so I decided to rent it out instead," he explained.

Jenny was quiet the rest of the way into Ottawa as if lost in her own thoughts.

They managed to find an underground parking spot at a local shopping centre and decided to visit the downtown market. The weather was warm, and the street was full of people. The outside restaurant patios were open, and they chose a place that offered salads, pita sandwiches, and large pitchers of iced tea.

Jenny looked around at all the people streaming by. "I really do miss this busyness. Sometimes when I have too much time to myself, it's easy for me to dwell on things."

Jake remembered Gertie's comment about how hard the last two years had been for Jenny, but he didn't know how to broach the subject. Maybe once she began to feel more comfortable with him, she would talk about what was making her so sad. He decided not to push the subject.

"What made you leave the city, Jake?" Jenny asked suddenly.

He surprised himself by not giving the reasons he normally cited by rote when asked this question—traffic, noise, and the need for solitude. Instead he spoke of his failed relationship. Of how he was unprepared when his former girlfriend had broken up with him. Of his feelings of rejection and his need for a new start.

"You keep referring to her as 'she'," Jenny said, quietly. "Maybe you'd feel better if you used her name when you talked about her. To acknowledge that she did in fact exist, that you loved her, and that you need to move on from her."

"Karen. Her name was Karen," Jake said, and felt as if by naming her, he had gained more control over his feelings toward her. She wasn't really the ogre he made her out to be, but it would be a long time, he realized, before he could think or say anything charitable about her.

After they finished their meal and had browsed the market, they went back to Jake's car and drove to Dow's Lake, the small man-made lake that feeds into the Rideau Canal. The local tulip festival was on, and they parked the car and watched the tourists as they snapped pictures of the beautiful blooms. They walked along the trails, enjoying the warmth of the sun and the peacefulness of the sparkling water.

A cyclist speeding along the walkway suddenly disrupted the tranquillity, and Jake instinctively reached for Jenny to move her out of the bike's path. Then, fearing that she might have been startled by his actions, he made light of the situation. "Just looking out for the little lady," he said in a John Wayne drawl.

"Your chivalry is much appreciated, but I swear that's the worst John Wayne imitation I've ever heard," Jenny said, laughing.

Jake thought how wonderful it was to hear that laughter as they continued along the walkway.

After an hour's walk, it was getting toward suppertime. Neither of them was hungry because of their late lunch, but they were getting tired and decided to return home.

"I really enjoyed the day, Jake," Jenny said. "If you're interested, there's a spring festival in town next weekend. They have it every May. The main street is closed off, and there are local artists and artisans showing their work. You could leave your car in the parking lot of my building, and we could walk around. You might even be able to find some artwork for your new house."

"Sounds like fun," Jake said. "It will be nice to see you again."

Jake let Jenny out in front of her apartment and drove to his house. It was still hard for him to think of it as a home, probably because of all the episodes he had experienced there. As his house came into view, he began to feel unsettled: this was the longest time he had spent away from it, and he couldn't dodge the feeling that his ghostly resident would not be pleased. But when he parked and entered the house, everything seemed to be as he had left it. He felt as if he had somehow dodged a bullet.

A silly thought, he chastised himself.

€€ €€ €€

18

Jake realized how much he was looking forward to the coming weekend with Jenny. They had, of course, exchanged e-mails on the home child Robert Wilson, but for the most part their investigation had hit a brick wall. He hoped there would be some answers soon to his various online inquiries.

He parked in Jenny's apartment lot that Saturday and watched as she walked down the outside flight of stairs to meet him. Jake guessed that she had been watching for him. He took this as a hopeful sign.

As they walked along the main street, he noticed a large number of people heading into the library.

"They have special events planned for today as

part of the festival," Jenny explained.

"I'm surprised you didn't have to work, Jenny."

She smiled shyly at him. "I asked for the day off once you accepted my invitation to join me for the festival."

They spent the day together walking around, viewing the various exhibits, and sampling the wares of the food vendors. Jake even managed to talk Jenny into getting a temporary tattoo. A good sport, she lined up with the parents and their children to wait, and chose a butterfly tattoo for her arm when it was her turn.

"This will cause some tongues to wag, no doubt," she laughed. "A bit daring for the local librarian, don't you think?"

"What? A butterfly tattoo? I was hoping you would be a little more adventurous. Maybe choose a skull and crossbones," Jake replied, winking at her.

Jenny invited him for supper. As he entered the apartment, Jake noticed that it was small, but comfortable. There were a number of antiques, including a huge oak sideboard in the dining area and some leather and oak chairs in the living room. She explained that her Aunt Gertrude had helped her outfit the apartment.

They had spaghetti with homemade sauce along with a wine from the local winery.

"That was wonderful, Jenny," Jake said, as he sipped his wine on the love seat in her living room.

She sat beside him and relaxed as he finally worked up the courage to put his arm around her shoulder.

They sat in silence like this for a long while, completely comfortable in each other's presence.

❦ ❦ ❦

19

Jake was busy the following week answering phone calls in response to his ad in the local paper for stall rentals. He had six spaces available.

On Wednesday he met with April Sorensen and her two teenaged daughters, Tanya and Ashley, and showed them the barn. April was a tall, thin woman with ash blond hair. Her daughters had the same build, colouring, and flawless complexion.

The good genes of the wealthy, he thought.

He explained to the Sorensens how his neighbour would provide square bales of hay for feed and how there was also a field, complete with jumps, where they could exercise and train their horses. Jake had

had the field mowed, and Fred had constructed the jumps after consulting the internet for competition specifications. Jake figured this would be a good selling point.

The Sorensens rented two of the stalls. By the end of the week, he had rented out two more stalls to a local family, and the sight of horse trailers in his yard suddenly made him feel better about having invested in the property. He would never be a farmer, but at least he was ensuring that the barn and the surrounding acreage were being put to good use.

The young women returned each day to feed and groom their horses, as well as to exercise them.

When things began to disappear mysteriously, Jake remembered the buzzing of the intercom from the barn that had interrupted his sleep several weeks ago.

He realized that the ghost's activity was not limited to the house. The disappearances started with small items such as water bottles, but gradually spread to larger items, including horse blankets and oat buckets. They would always show up again, but never in their proper place.

"I think you have a poltergeist, Jake," said Tanya Sorensen one day. "I hope it's a good-natured one," she laughed.

So far it has been. Let's hope it stays that way, Jake thought.

He felt uneasy. He did not like the idea of other

people being caught up unwittingly in this sphere of supernatural activity.

20

Over the next few weeks, Jake and Jenny saw each other on the weekends. She confided to him one evening that her gaunt appearance was not natural for her. She had lost thirty pounds over the past two years.

"My dad died two years ago. He was in his early sixties so his death was a shock to us. He and my mom had just returned from their annual winter trip to Florida. Dad was shovelling out the driveway so he could get the car in. He collapsed and died in the ambulance en route to the hospital.

"My mother sold our family home and moved to St. Catharines a year after Dad's death. She rents an apartment there. She's from that area and still has friends there. I see her when I can. I have two older sisters, one in Vancouver and one in Montreal, but they were much older when I was born, and we were never close. We exchange Christmas greetings and that's about it. So I feel a bit adrift: as if I've lost my whole family, except for Aunt Gertrude, of course, who's been very good to me since I moved back from Ottawa."

"I'm very sorry, Jenny," Jake said simply.

"I went for grief counselling after my father's death, and intellectually I can acknowledge the various stages of grief they teach you and how you gradually progress from denial to acceptance. But grief is a very personal thing. I've discovered that for me it's a visceral reaction.

"And before I could come to terms with my dad's death, my best friend since grade school, Sarah, was killed in a car accident. The other driver was texting and didn't look up in time to avoid the collision. I guess it happens quite often, but what do you say to yourself when someone you care about dies in their mid-thirties and the driver at fault walks away unharmed? What good does it do to talk about the stages of grief then?"

Jake knew these were rhetorical questions. He stroked her hair as she cried quietly on his shoulder.

As the weeks passed and they gained each other's

trust, their relationship developed into intimacy. To Jake's delight, Jenny laughed more often and seemed to be gradually emerging back into life. In turn, Jake felt wanted and needed for the first time in a long while. He discovered it was okay to be a nice guy despite Karen's dismissiveness.

Jenny even joined him when she could at Betty's restaurant on his Tuesday shopping trips. Betty was thrilled to see Jake with a female companion— especially a hometown girl of whom she approved— and was also eager to have someone else to fatten up.

Jake's only concern was that he had not told Jenny about the episodes at his house. And despite her jokes that the town gossips would brand her a "scarlet woman" when they saw him emerging at an early hour from her apartment, he never invited her to stay overnight at his house.

He feared there might be an escalation of events. He did not want her harmed.

❧ ❧ ❧

21

The e-mail from the Quarriers Society came in mid-June.

Dear Mr. Hall,

We are sorry for the delay in responding, but we have a backlog of requests.

Regarding your inquiry concerning Robert Wilson from the Quarrier Homes in Scotland, this is to confirm that Robert entered Canada at the age of ten and was sent to the Fitzgeralds' farm in eastern Ontario. I understand from your e-mail that you tracked Robert through the 1921 census, but could not find a death certificate. Unfortunately, we have no record of Robert later than 1925, when, according to his file, he was adopted by the Fitzgeralds.

Regarding Robert's siblings, there were in fact two younger brothers. Jonathan Wilson came to Canada at age eight and was sent to a farm in the Peterborough area. Cecil Wilson came to Canada at age six. He was adopted by a family in Westport. Regrettably, we do not have any further records on Jonathan and Cecil....

Jake recognized the familiar pattern repeated in the history of the Wilson children: siblings were often separated, never to see one another again. He had also read that many Canadian families claimed to have adopted their home children to avoid further inquiries by the authorities. In 1925, Robert would have reached the age of eighteen and would no longer have been indentured to the Fitzgeralds. Jake expected that the adoption—if, in fact, it was official—was a means of ensuring Robert's ongoing servitude on the farm.

But at least the e-mail had provided him with the names of Robert's siblings. Jake updated his online posting to include a reference to the two brothers and once again appealed for information from anyone who was a descendant or knew of the family.

The episodes escalated in frequency after Jake received the e-mail from the Quarriers Society. His journal was becoming full of entries. Whenever he entered a room, Jake would find the cats staring and hissing as if at an unseen presence. His cell phone was constantly moved, as was the photo of Robert Wilson. He had begun putting the picture in his desk drawer at night, but it was always on his bedside stand in the morning.

The long wait for information on Robert's descendants continued, as Jake became more and more frustrated at his inability to get the right answers. Even Jenny was starting to display this same frustration. She had begun new searches under the name Robert Fitzgerald in the event that he had been officially adopted by the Fitzgeralds and had taken their name. But she could find no death certificate under this name either.

⋐⋙ ⋐⋙ ⋐⋙

22

Jenny was concerned about Jake's reluctance to have her stay in his house. She had made some short visits in the daytime, but Jake was always tense in the evenings and made excuses why they should go to her apartment. She didn't like secrets, especially with someone she cared for so much.

She decided to force the issue on a Friday evening when she knew he would be working at his computer on his latest article. She arrived at his door with takeout food. She also carried a small overnight bag, which she left in the hall.

"I thought I'd surprise you with Thai food in case you haven't made your bologna sandwiches yet."

"Come in. It's great to see you. I haven't eaten yet."

Although his tone was welcoming, Jenny could see how his shoulders had tightened, which she recognized as a sign of stress.

After paying proper attention to Callie and Licorice, who had come to the door to see who was visiting, Jenny made her way to the kitchen and put the takeout containers on the table while Jake set out plates and utensils.

"Would you like a glass of wine?" he asked Jenny, holding up a bottle of chardonnay.

"I think we both should have a glass, Jake. No more nonsense. I want you to tell me what's going on in this house and why you don't want me to spend any amount of time here. I know it's got something to do with the home child Robert Wilson because you get tense every time I mention his name. Please tell me what's going on."

"I didn't mean to shut you out, Jenny. Let's eat first and then we can talk about this afterward."

After they had finished eating, they took their wine to the living room where they sat together on the couch.

"Several months ago, I began to experience activities in this house. At first I just thought my mind was playing tricks on me, but the episodes—as I started to think of them—became so frequent that I couldn't ignore them any more."

He then described the feeling of being watched, the hand- and footprints, the unexplained noises, the displacement of objects, and the acceleration of incidents since he had found out the identity of Robert Wilson's siblings. He also told her that the previous occupants of the house thought it was cursed.

"I think this is the point at which you start avoiding eye contact with me and make a run for the door," Jake said, laughing uneasily.

"I admit it's a lot to take in, Jake, but I believe that you're completely guileless: that's the reason I care for you so much. If you say you've experienced these things, I see no reason to question your judgment ... or your sanity, if that's what you're afraid of."

Jake heaved a sigh of relief and felt much better having shared his burden. But he was still worried about the escalation of the episodes. In his research he had noted that violence could occur as part of an escalation. He explained this to Jenny. She asked if there had been any indication of violence so far or any indication that the ghost of Robert Wilson wanted anything more than to be reunited with his family.

"No," Jake admitted, "but I'm still worried about your safety in this house."

"I don't think there's any cause for worry, Jake. And I really would like to help you resolve this, if that's possible."

"And you don't think I'm off my rocker?" Jake asked, still uneasy.

Jenny smiled and offered him her hand. "Of course not. What's that line from *Hamlet* that everyone quotes? Something about more things in heaven and earth..."

Jake slept peacefully that night in Jenny's arms. She stirred first in the morning and reached over to playfully poke his shoulder. "I don't mean to complain, Jake, but this lumpy mattress has got to go if you want me as a house guest."

"I promise to replace the mattress. And I'll even buy a new one from Sears. I won't try to find a second-hand one from your aunt's shop," Jake said, as he gently brushed the hair from her eyes.

"Well, in that case, how about making me a permanent house guest? I know I'm being forward, but I may be an old maid before you get up the courage to ask me to move in with you. Besides, I'd rather wrangle ghosts out here than stay in that apartment and listen to the traffic and late-night drunks from the pub. So what do you say? Too brazen for you?"

He laughed and said, "First things first. I get a new mattress and then I help you move in here. As long as you're sure that you'll feel safe here."

"I'm sure," she said simply and that was the end of the discussion.

⋘ ⋘ ⋘

23

Jenny lay awake the following night in her apartment and started second-guessing herself, as she often did on restless nights. She wondered if she had been too precipitous in suggesting that she move in with Jake. It was in her nature to be more cautious, more conservative. But she felt good with Jake and more comfortable than she had felt with anyone in a long time. She knew he was still recovering from a failed relationship, but she sensed that he cared deeply for her. They had been together for only a few months, but Jenny still believed that it was the right move for both of them.

The next three weeks passed in a flurry of activity

as she prepared for the move. She survived by making numerous lists to stay organized. She had managed to sublet the apartment to someone who worked in the nearby coffee shop, and her Aunt Gertrude had offered her the use of her old pickup truck, which would accommodate her sparse furnishings in one or two trips. All the appliances stayed in the apartment, so the only really heavy item to move was her oak sideboard.

Jenny had no sense of foreboding: she was looking forward to the move.

❧ ❧ ❧

24

Jake had just finished talking to Jenny on his cell phone about her upcoming move on the weekend when he glanced out the kitchen window and saw Tanya Sorensen riding her horse Ariel into the yard. She dismounted quickly, looking very upset. Jake hurried to meet her in the barn.

"Is something wrong, Tanya?" he asked with concern as he saw how pale she looked.

"I took a tumble," she said, "but it could have been much worse. Ariel caught her hoof in some boards. She could have broken her leg, but she reared up in time. That's when I fell."

"Are you okay?"

"Yes, but I don't understand how it happened. Remember when I first came here with my mother and sister to look at the stall? You told me there was an abandoned well on the property but that it had been covered up with new boards. Well, the boards were all torn up and thrown aside. Who could have done that?"

Jake shook his head, not knowing what to say, and asked if he could call Tanya's mother to take her home. Then he called Fred and explained what had happened.

"I got rid of the old, rotten boards when I built the new platform, Jake. The new planks were solid. I don't know why anyone would tear them up. If there's any vandalism around here, it's usually teenagers playing mailbox baseball and knocking over the boxes." He agreed to come over immediately.

When Fred arrived, Jake climbed into the passenger seat of his pickup. As they approached the far side of the field that had been set up for exercising the horses, Jake could see splintered boards lying on the ground near the old well.

"Someone's gone to a lot of trouble to destroy this platform," Fred said, as they left his truck to survey the damage. "They must have pried the boards up and then smashed them. Funny, though. I can't see any pry marks. Normally you'd see where the claw of the hammer has gripped the wood. I can replace the platform, but I'm wondering if I should check with

Ed Sewell. He has a local construction business. Maybe he can suggest an alternative, depending on how deep the well is. It might be possible to fill it in with a backhoe to seal it. Are you okay with me giving him a call?"

"That would be great, Fred. I find the price tends to go higher when they learn you're new to the area.

Maybe you can get him to quote some ballpark figures for filling it in."

"I'd be glad to. In the meantime, I'll put some plywood over the well and drive some stakes to rope it off. Still puzzles me, though, why someone would do this."

Jake had Fred drop him off at the house and then started working on his latest article. He was about three-quarters of the way through it when his cell phone rang. It was Fred telling him that Sewell would have a look at the well, but it might be a couple of weeks because his crew was tied up in townhouse construction.

"That's okay, Fred, I'll warn everyone to stay away from it, and the plywood should keep any wildlife out."

Jake finished the draft of his article and went to the kitchen to get a late-night snack. He was taking some milk from the fridge when he happened to glance at the fridge door while he was closing it. There was a sheet of paper held in place by a magnet. He had not put it there. The message on it read:

As round as an apple,
As deep as a cup,
And all the king's horses
Can't fill it up.

He knew it must be a nursery rhyme, but he couldn't place it. With a sense of foreboding, he went back to his desk and fired up his computer to do a Google search.

The poem was from a book of Mother Goose nursery rhymes. Its title was "The Well".

When Tanya had first told him of the damage at the well site, he was skeptical that the destruction had been performed by human hands. After reading the nursery rhyme, Jake believed that the ghost was responsible for the damage. If so, this meant that its sphere of influence was once again expanding.

❦ ❦ ❦

25

Jake awoke the next morning with a feeling of apprehension. He realized what he was expecting to find in the well—the bones of Robert Wilson—and he thought for a moment of asking Fred to help him descend its walls with the help of a rope and pulley so he could examine its contents. But he knew he had no logical explanation to give to Fred for wanting to do this, especially since Sewell's crew would be coming to examine the well in two weeks. He would just have to wait.

It was the day of Jenny's move, and he busied himself with the preparations. The two men who worked part-time for Jenny's Aunt Gertrude had accepted the moving job. They would use her aunt's pickup truck to move everything from Jenny's apartment. Jake would stay at his house to await their arrival and direct them on the placement of the furniture and boxes. Her oak sideboard would go in the dining room, and her antique chairs would have place of honour in the living room. The rest of her living room furniture would fit in an adjacent room they had decided to make into a TV room and den. There was a smaller room near the kitchen that overlooked the yard and had probably once served as a breakfast nook. Jenny had decided to use this room as an office, so her desk and chair would go there. Her bed and bedroom furniture would be placed in one of the spare bedrooms that Jake had not yet furnished. He hoped that Jenny's mother might be able to visit them at Christmas, and this would serve as her bedroom. The boxes would be stored in a back summer kitchen—not in the attic, which Jake still avoided—until Jenny had time to unpack everything. Once the movers had made their final trip, Jenny would follow in her car, bringing china, plants, and other fragile items with her.

Jenny had already announced her plans to re-take control of the attic. She would have Fred plug up any holes he could find to keep the mice out, and she was making inquiries as to which local pest control companies would remove the mice with live traps and re-locate them at least a mile away to discourage their return. In the interim, she had saturated cotton balls with peppermint oil—as instructed by Aunt Gertrude—and placed them throughout the attic. Apparently, mice were repelled by its smell.

By mid-afternoon, the move was complete, and Jake marvelled at the fact that his nearly-empty house now felt much more like a home. And the happiness he felt at having Jenny with him made him forget Robert Wilson for a while.

They took a break from unpacking around 7 PM to have a late supper. Jake poured Jenny a glass of wine and insisted that she put her feet up and relax in their new den. He placed garlic bread in the oven to warm, boiled water on the stove for Olivieri tortellini, and mixed pesto and vinaigrette dressing for the sauce. He set the table and went to tell Jenny that everything was ready. He found her looking through his DVD collection. They had discovered early in their relationship that they shared a love for old, campy science fiction movies, as well as TV detective series.

She smiled up at him when he entered the room. "You have some great stuff here. Some of it I didn't even realize was available." She had a copy of *The Avengers* in her hand: not the Marvel comic book heroes, but the British series with Diana Rigg as Mrs. Peel. As she moved to put the DVD back on the shelf, something tumbled to the floor. It was the photograph of Robert Wilson, once again displaced from Jake's desk, as if to remind them both that they still had work to do on his behalf.

As he served the pasta and garlic bread, Jake talked to Jenny about the vandalism of the well and showed her the nursery rhyme he had found on his refrigerator door. He told her he believed that the remains of Robert Wilson would be found in the well.

"If that's the case," Jenny said, "I wonder if their discovery will finally bring closure for his spirit."

"I don't think so," Jake said. "We're still no closer to identifying any of Robert's living relatives, and I don't think there'll be any true closure until he's reunited with his family."

"Then we'll just have to keep trying to find his descendants. Maybe if we post some new messages..."

Jenny's reply was interrupted by a crash from the den. When they went to investigate, they discovered the shards of her broken wine glass, the red wine pooling like blood on the hardwood floor.

Just like the episode in the shower, Jake thought.

❦ ❦ ❦

26

The episodes did not increase in frequency after Jenny moved into the house, as Jake had feared. Aside from the shattered wine glass, there had been only one incident involving Jenny herself. She had awakened early one morning to use the bathroom and had glimpsed what appeared to be a vapour behind her when she glanced in the bathroom mirror. She accepted the incident with her usual calm demeanour, trying to determine if there might be a logical explanation, although she found none. For his part, Jake felt both relieved that someone else was finally understanding what he had been experiencing over the past months, and apprehensive for Jenny because she now had been drawn into it.

In addition to hearing overhead footsteps, they both had detected a faint smell coming from the locked attic. Jake attributed it to the peppermint oil, but Jenny didn't think the smell originated with this oil. Although she couldn't place the scent, she associated it with childhood memories of her grandmother.

They were both relieved when word finally came from Fred that Sewell and his crew would be able to examine the well site the following morning. In response to Jake's questioning, Fred assured him that one of Sewell's crew would be descending into the well to determine its depth and how best it could be filled to avoid posing a future hazard.

Jenny was working at the library the next morning when Fred came to pick up Jake. He was on edge and did not respond when Fred said jokingly: "You're awfully anxious to see what's down there. You expecting to find buried treasure?"

Sewell and his crew were already at the site, having been given directions by Fred on using a back road to the farm. He looked Jake up and down when he stepped from the cab of the truck, registering the fact that he was a stranger. Fred made the introductions, and Sewell reluctantly shook Jake's proffered hand. Jake half-expected Sewell to rub his hand off on his jeans afterward to avoid catching a communicable disease, but instead he turned abruptly and started issuing instructions to his crew. They removed the makeshift covering that Fred had built and then began to lower one of the workmen down using a winch.

"Shouldn't you send a canary down first?" Fred joked.

No one laughed.

As the man descended, he tested his footholds on the side of the well and assured himself that the wall would not crumble. There was a jolt on the rope and a thud as he called up to say he had reached the bottom. Jake waited impatiently for the man to pace off the well to determine its size.

"Okay, I'm coming up," he finally yelled, his voice echoing off the walls. When he surfaced from the well and was detaching the rope from his work belt, he said: "It's only about twelve feet deep so we shouldn't have any problem filling it with a backhoe."

Jake could contain himself no longer. "What's down there?" he asked with an urgency in his voice.

The worker looked at him as if he were particularly slow, even for someone new to the area. "There's nothing down there," he said finally. "It's just a dried-up well."

When Jake called Jenny at the library later that morning, it was readily apparent from his tone that he was discouraged. He tried to joke about it: "I guess logic doesn't play a huge role in the spirit world. Otherwise, Robert Wilson's ghost wouldn't have made such a big deal about the well. It seems to be taking a rather serpentine path to discovery."

"Let's declare a moratorium on talk of Robert Wilson for this evening," Jenny said. "How about dinner and a movie in Brockville after I get home from work?"

They had not spent an evening out since Jenny had moved in, as if by tacit agreement they were reluctant to leave the house unattended, and they were overdue for a break. Jake readily agreed to the suggestion.

After watching the latest blockbuster movie—which they both thoroughly enjoyed because it was a lot of noise and confusion that didn't require anything in the way of profound thought—they went to the sports bar that served the best hamburgers in the city. They sat at a table at the back to avoid the noise from the television and bar.

"I nominate myself the designated driver," Jenny said as they looked at the menu, "so go ahead and get whatever you want to drink."

"You're just trying to ply me with liquor and have your way with me," Jake replied, laughing.

Jenny shook her head in mock disgust. Just then, the waitress appeared to take their orders. Judging from the smirk she tried to suppress as she asked them what they would like to drink, she had overheard Jake's remark.

After the waitress had taken their orders, Jake—looking embarrassed—quickly changed the subject, asking Jenny about her mother and whether she would approve of their relationship.

"Don't worry about my mother," Jenny said. "She'll be very pleased that her daughter finally decided to forgo the convention of marriage and 'live in sin'. Mom prides herself on being a free spirit. She thinks I'm too uptight.

"She loved to tell me stories of the 60s and 70s when I was a child: how she read Daniel Ellsberg's papers on the Vietnam War; watched the televised Watergate hearings; and organized an impromptu parade when Nixon announced his resignation.

"I remember she listened non-stop to Bob Dylan and Neil Young when I was growing up. Unfortunately, she also had a thing for Leonard Cohen. She had most of his songs memorized and sang along off-key to his records. I was amazed that she didn't name me Suzanne or Marianne. She even went to one of his concerts in Montreal a few years back. I never had the heart to tell her I thought Leonard Cohen sounded like he had severed vocal chords. To this day, she thinks I really like his singing.

"When she's a bit tipsy, she likes to listen to the song 'San Francisco' and talk about how wonderful a time it was in the 60s when anything seemed possible.

"She says it's all different now. No optimism post-9/11. She describes it as the *24* mentality—you know, from that TV show with Kiefer Sutherland as Jack Bauer—where state-sanctioned torture and murder is the new American way. She doesn't figure Canada's much different under Harper because he accused his critics of being soft on terrorism when they raised the issue of prisoners being tortured in Afghanistan.

"I think secretly she still prides herself on being a 'radical.' But then again, she's probably not that far off in her judgment of current events.

"I guess I've always felt a little overwhelmed by my mother. Temperament-wise, I was always much closer to my dad. They were exact opposites, but they loved each other dearly. He was a bit conservative and very much by the book. When he died, I felt as if I had lost my sounding board and my best friend."

This was the longest that Jenny had talked about her family but, sensing her sadness, he decided it was time to lighten the mood. "Your mom would probably be horrified, then, that I'm a closet Jack Bauer fan. Maybe we can keep that under wraps if she visits us at Christmas. I'd really like to meet her. She sounds as irreverent as your Aunt Gertrude, whom I'm very fond of, by the way."

Jenny grew animated. "That would be wonderful, Jake. Having Mom here at Christmas, and maybe having Aunt Gertrude over for Christmas Eve or

Christmas dinner. I think they'd both really enjoy that."

And I will too, Jake thought, *provided there is no ghost to disturb her holiday. We need to resolve this situation now. It's gone on far too long.*

❦ ❦ ❦

27

The summer passed quickly. Jenny was busy with her work at the library and with her weekend activities, including organizing puppet shows for children, adult literary workshops, and events for seniors. She also attended women's book club meetings twice a month, although judging by her uncharacteristic bouts of giggling when he drove her home after these meetings, Jake suspected that the ladies spent more time sampling wine than discussing books.

Jake had finished the Armchair Economist series and had two additional contracts from the same publisher. In his spare time, he harvested the gardens with the help of Jeremy McFarlane. After keeping enough for himself and Jenny, he sold the surplus to local restaurants, and also donated vegetables to the food bank.

One weekend in early September after the cucumbers had been harvested, Jenny invited Gertie and Betty for a pickling session. She had also bought peaches and strawberries to make jam. Jenny had never made pickles and preserves so she thought it would be a good time to learn from the older women.

Gertie arrived with her huge enamel pots and Mason jars, and Betty brought large wooden bowls that had belonged to her mother. They would use these bowls for chopping up the cucumbers and onions. It was a festive atmosphere as the smell of simmering fruits and vegetables filled the kitchen.

"It's nice to share these recipes," Gertie said. "Everyone has to learn sometime. I learned from my mother. She was a great cook, but even Mother had some failures. She used to tell me about the time she tried a new recipe for dill pickles. She added too much alum and they weren't fit to eat. That was the first and last time that Mother experimented with a new recipe."

Jenny nodded as she sliced onions in a large bowl for mustard pickles. "I remember your stories, Aunt Gertrude, from when I was young. I always thought it was wonderful how you carried on Grandma's traditions."

Jake poked his head into the kitchen to see how the women were doing. "Speaking of family traditions, Jenny, did you get a chance to mention Christmas?"

"Thanks for reminding me, Jake. Mom is coming for a week at Christmas, and we'd love to have you join us for Christmas dinner, Aunt Gertrude. We want you and Fred to join us as well, Betty, if you haven't already made other plans."

Both ladies readily agreed. Gertie was buoyant at the thought of seeing her younger sister again, and Betty, who had grown up with Iris Campbell, was touched by the fact that Jenny and Jake had included her and Fred in the invitation.

Jake helped Gertie and Betty carry out some jars of pickles and preserves that Jenny insisted they take. Gertie touched his arm as they reached her car. "Thanks for taking the sadness from her eyes, Jake. I haven't seen her this happy in a long while."

"It's mutual, Gertie. She's very special to me."

⋇⋇⋇ ⋇⋇⋇ ⋇⋇⋇

28

It was early one morning in late September that Jake received a call from Jeremy McFarlane.

"I was repairing a fence between our two farms, Jake. I didn't think you'd mind if I went on your property to fix it so I could keep my cattle away from your field. The damnedest thing happened, though. When I was digging the hole for the new fence post, I hit something with my shovel. It looks like a bone. It must be some kind of grave, but it's too far from your house to be the remains of a family pet. I don't like to do any more digging without you being here. Can you meet me at the northeast corner of your property?"

When Jake joined his neighbour at the fence line of his property, he thought he already knew what they would find. A preliminary excavation of the shallow grave revealed bones that looked to be of human origin. Jake called the local detachment of the Ontario Provincial Police, asking for guidance.

OPP officers arrived with the local coroner after being contacted by Jake, and cordoned off the area to avoid further disturbance. They, in turn, contacted the RCMP to determine whether a criminal investigation was warranted. Jake and Jeremy were relegated to the role of onlookers.

Jake soon found out that the laws governing the discovery of human remains are complex in nature, cover both federal and provincial jurisdictions, and vary according to the province in which the remains are found. He learned, for example, that in Ontario the OPP is required to advise the nearest First Nation band council when human remains are discovered.

Although he assumed that the remains were those of Robert Wilson, he faced the dilemma of explaining this to the authorities without discussing the supernatural episodes that had led him to this conclusion. In the end, he and Jenny decided to show the police the photo of Robert Wilson, describe the research they had done to establish that Robert was a home child who had come to Canada in 1917 to work at the Fitzgerald farm, and advise the police that they had been unable to locate his death certificate.

They explained their interest in him as part of their research into the history of the house.

The coroner was able to identify the remains as belonging to a teenager, aged sixteen to eighteen. Subsequent examination of the bones by a consulting forensic archaeologist determined that they were approximately ninety years old, which would fit with the time frame in which Robert Wilson had been a resident at the Fitzgerald farm. There were several fractures in the bones, but there was no evidence to suggest foul play as the cause of death. The forensic archaeologist indicated that the fractures were consistent with those that would have been sustained in a fall.

Once contacted and advised of the probable identity of the deceased, the First Nations council agreed that the investigation could proceed without its further involvement.

The bones were retained by the authorities while they contacted Police Scotland to enlist help in determining whether there were any living relatives who would claim the remains. Jake asked that his telephone number and e-mail address be provided to any relatives the police managed to locate.

The authorities succeeded where Jake had failed, probably because they had a wider communication network at their disposal. In mid-November, Jake received an e-mail from Colin Wilson, explaining that he was the grandson of Cecil Wilson, who had emigrated from Scotland as a home child, but had subsequently returned to his birthplace. Colin had been contacted by the local police constabulary when inquiries were made from Canada regarding the discovery of what were presumed to be his great-uncle Robert Wilson's bones. Colin indicated that he would be travelling to Canada to arrange for the repatriation of the remains once they had been released from police custody. He said he would like to meet with Jake, who, he understood from communicating with the Canadian authorities, was essential in identifying the remains of his great-uncle.

❧ ❧ ❧

29

On a day in late November, Jake and Jenny waited in the arrivals area of the Ottawa airport. Colin Wilson had cleared Customs in Toronto and was due shortly on the Canadian leg of his flight. When the arrival of the flight was announced, Jake expected to see a short, florid-faced man with a dour expression emerge from the plane. To his surprise, Colin Wilson was a tall, pleasant-looking man who strode forward with his hand extended to greet the two of them.

So much for stereotypes, Jake chastised himself.

Colin would stay with them while he met with the

local authorities to see if Robert Wilson's remains could be released for cremation. He would require a certificate of cremation to bring the ashes back to Scotland.

They had debated what to tell Colin regarding his great-uncle. They saw no point in adding to his grief by explaining how harshly they believed Robert Wilson had been treated by Abraham Fitzgerald. Colin had already been advised by the police of the findings of the forensic archaeologist that the fractures in Robert Wilson's bones were consistent with those normally suffered in a fall. Jake and Jenny did not like to consider the alternative: that Robert had suffered a final beating that resulted in his death.

They also saw no point in mentioning the supernatural episodes they had experienced in their house. As they had done with the police, they would advise Colin simply that their research into the history of the house had led them to the discovery of Robert's identity.

After supper, Colin shared some documents with them that he had amassed in helping his father trace his family history. Jake asked Colin why he had not responded to his internet postings asking for information on Robert Wilson.

"My children tell me I'm hopeless when it comes to the internet. They've talked to me about websites and search engines and all that good stuff, but I'm afraid I'm a neophyte when it comes to using the internet. Even sending e-mail is a challenge for me, but I've learned how to do it because I need to use e-mail at work."

"If you like, we'll show you some of the internet research sites while you're here with us," Jake said. "It might help you piece together the story of your grandfather's and his brothers' migration from Scotland."

"I'd like that," Colin replied. "I did a lot of legwork searching through physical records. As you know, all three of the Wilson children came to Canada from the Quarrier homes. The children were separated, but my great-uncle Jonathan and my grandfather Cecil were able to reunite when they returned to Scotland and bought small farms in Renfrewshire County. That's where the Quarrier homes were located—in Bridge of Weir. My grandfather tried relentlessly to find news of Robert, but Grandfather died without ever seeing or hearing from Robert again. My dad, Joseph Wilson, took up the search, but he was never able to track Robert beyond the Fitzgerald farm.

"My great-grandparents had a daughter after their three sons were sent to Canada, but she contracted tuberculosis and died at an early age. She was buried in a pauper's grave, and my great-grandparents died penniless and were buried in the cemetery of a local poorhouse. With my help, my father was able to locate the graves and have their remains exhumed and buried in the same cemetery plot as my great-uncle Jonathan and my grandfather Cecil. If I can get clear of the red tape here, I'd like to bury Robert's ashes in the same plot so he can finally be reunited with his parents and siblings."

Shortly after, feeling the effects of jet lag, Colin retired to the guest bedroom.

"This is all so sad," Jenny said, as she sat on the couch and rested her head on Jake's shoulder.

"It is sad, Jenny, but at least we've played a part in reuniting the family. I hope Robert will finally be at peace."

After a week, despite the fact that there were still unanswered questions, Colin Wilson was finally able to persuade the Canadian authorities that he would take responsibility for the remains. The coroner had been unable to determine the exact cause of death, and it was unlikely at this late date, with all the principals deceased, that it would ever be known. Colin arranged for the cremation of the remains and obtained the necessary documentation to return them to Scotland. He would keep the urn in his home until the grave of Robert's family could be re-opened in the spring.

As he shook hands and said good-bye to Jake and Jenny, he thanked them again for their hospitality and wished them all the best in the future. "I'll let you know when the burial takes place," he said before joining the line to board his plane.

Jake and Jenny felt both relief and emptiness as they entered their now-quiet home. It had been a long, hard journey of discovery, but it seemed finally to be at an end.

❧ ❧ ❧

30

The next morning, Jake was working on his computer, about to submit his latest article. He noticed that some text had suddenly appeared at the end of his e-mail. Recalling the earlier incident in which his e-mail to his editor had been "hijacked," he called Jenny over, thinking that it was probably a thank you and farewell from Robert Wilson.

Jenny stood behind him with her hands on his shoulders, and the two of them read the message together. It was not at all what they had expected.

I am thankful to you for allowing Robert, my home child, to return to his beloved Scotland and his rightful family.

He was a wonderful boy. I taught him to read and do numbers at his little desk when he wasn't labouring for my husband. At night I read him stories until he fell asleep. I like to think that I gave him a few moments of happiness while he lived with us.

But I am guilty of the sin of omission. Because I feared my husband, I did not intervene in his harsh treatment of Robert, even though it made me sick at heart.

Robert used to hide from Abraham in the barn, and then finally he tried to run away because he could take no more abuse. But he fell into the old well on our property.

Abraham claimed that Robert was already dead when he found him. He swore me to secrecy on pain of death for fear he might be called into account. Together we hid the fact of Robert's death. There were no further inquiries from the authorities because we said that we had adopted Robert. I was guilty once again of sin by complying with my husband's wishes.

My husband boarded up the old well and deposited poor Robert's body in an unmarked grave on our property. No minister attended, and poor Robert had no proper burial. The only thing I had remaining of him was the picture I took with our box camera when my husband was not at home. I hid it in the old photograph album of my family.

Abraham cast a shadow and curse upon our farm and others nearby. I lost my beloved son Jonathan a year later when he fell through the ice and drowned in the creek out back. Other deaths followed.

You are a kind man who cared about a long-dead child you never knew. I pray that you have ended the curse. I know that you have allowed me atonement for my sins. Perhaps my soul will suffer less in the next world than it has in this one.

With my eternal gratitude,
Alma Fitzgerald

"I never once considered that it was anyone other than Robert in this house," Jake said. "I just assumed that it was because he had unfinished business: he needed to connect with his own family in Scotland."

Jenny was shaking her head, as if to dispel the shock. "I remember you told me once that, according to what you'd read, spirits can linger behind for a number of reasons. You said that one of the reasons is that they have unfinished business, but I think you also mentioned another—fear of the afterlife. It makes sense that Alma Fitzgerald feared judgment: she said twice in the letter that she had sinned."

"I guess it makes a certain amount of sense when I think of it," Jake said. "It started with the feeling of being watched and then I discovered the muddy boots and the hand- and footprints outside. They could easily have belonged to a female. And the figure I saw hovering near my bed that I thought was a child could also have been female. I recall Lorne Ramsay saying that his mother had referred to Mrs. Fitzgerald as a petite woman.

"The other pieces seem to fit too. The constant reappearance of the photograph makes sense now that I understand its importance to Mrs. Fitzgerald. And I can also see the significance of the well."

"I've just realized something else," Jenny said. "That odour we detected, but couldn't identify. When Lorne told us the story of his mother's conversation with Mrs. Fitzgerald, he talked about how his mother watched her wringing her handkerchief in her hands. Remember Lorne said his mother could smell lily of the valley? I bet that's what we've been smelling too, coming from the attic. I associated the scent with my grandmother, and I remember now how she always wore fragrance when she dressed up for church."

"It's going to take us a while to wrap our heads around this. We were so certain that it was Robert's ghost that finally led us to the discovery of the grave. But regardless, I hope Mrs. Fitzgerald is at peace now," Jake said, "and that she's right about the curse being over. I'd like us to live a normal life in this house. And I'd like to think that the creek will never claim another victim."

"No argument there," Jenny replied, hugging

Jake and watching as the last of Alma Fitzgerald's words disappeared from the screen.

❦ ❦ ❦

Epilogue

On a rainy spring day when the ground had finally thawed, Colin Wilson, along with his father and children, stood in an old church cemetery and watched as the urn containing the ashes of Robert Frederick Wilson was placed in the ground and he was finally reunited with his family. The elderly minister spoke a few words of benediction.

After the ceremony, they politely accepted the minister's offer to join him for a cup of tea.

As he was about to close the door to the manse, Colin glanced back at the grave. He fancied that he saw a single ray of sunlight penetrating the gloom before the clouds once again eclipsed the sky.

❧ ❧ ❧

Afterword

More than a decade ago, I was visiting a small museum in Brockville when I saw a child's bed with an iron headboard and an old worn suitcase. There was a typed notice on the wall explaining that the items had belonged to a "home child"—in this case, a young girl—and detailing the hardships these children faced in leaving their homeland and moving to Canada. This was my first encounter with the term "home child," but the stark images of the bed and suitcase stayed with me all these years. I couldn't begin to imagine how abandoned and desolate this little girl must have felt to leave her family and travel on a huge ship to a new land.

When I decided to write a novel in my retirement, the home children came to mind as a natural subject.

I am not a historian and would have felt out of my depth in writing a historical account of the home children, especially since there are already a number of excellent books on this subject. So instead I decided to write a supernatural novel.

While I've tried to be as accurate as possible in providing historical details based on my research, this is in the end a work of fiction. For the sake of the story, I've invented some of the details and have shortened the time frame for the release and repatriation of Robert Wilson's remains.

Acknowledgments

I would like to thank my husband, Mike McCann, for his encouragement, his input on details such as the inclusion of home children in censuses of the time, his reading of the manuscript and suggested revisions, and his technical expertise and assistance in the publication of this novel. Thanks, Mike, for believing there could be two authors in one family. Now if only I can learn your discipline in writing to a schedule!

I would like to acknowledge the part that home children have played in the history of Canada. At least ten per cent of Ontario's population—some estimates are as high as twelve per cent—are descendants of home children, who thrived and made their indelible mark on this country despite the hardships they suffered.

There are many resources for those who would

like to do further research on home children. For the history of child migration from the Quarrier homes in Scotland, testimonies from individual home children, and an extensive bibliography as well as links to other relevant websites, please see *the golden bridge* site on the internet at http://content.iriss.org.uk/goldenbridge/index.html. I consulted this site for the history of the Quarrier homes and such details as the items packed in the trunk of a home child.

Another invaluable resource is the Library and Archives Canada internet website at http://www.bac-lac.gc.ca/. It contains digitized copies of Canadian census information, as well as birth, marriage, and death records. It also contains records on the home children who emigrated from the United Kingdom to Canada, and passenger lists for the ships that brought them here. The 1921 census referenced in this novel has been released by Library and Archives Canada to Ancestry.ca/. It may currently be accessed through their internet website at http://www.ancestry.ca.

I was also fortunate in having been referred to Anna Magnusson's excellent book entitled *Quarriers Story* (Toronto: Dundurn Press, 2006), which provides a balanced account of what William Quarrier hoped to achieve in the way of a better life for the 7,000 children sent to Canada from his homes.

A special thanks goes to Melanie Robertson-King and to her husband Donald King for providing me with a copy of Ms. Magnusson's book and for sharing their insights into what it was like for many home children in Canada.

I would also like to thank Dave Wells for discussing the subject of home children with me when we met in Brockville and for providing me with a list of local home child contacts.

I appreciate their guidance. Any errors of interpretation in this novel are solely mine.

The information on ghosts is compiled from various sites because there is a wealth of material available on the internet. For example, the reasons why spirits remain earthbound are discussed at http://theshadowlands.net/ghost/stay.htm. The signs of haunting are outlined in http://paranormal. about.com/od/ghosthuntinggeninfo/a/aa060704. htm. My apologies to paranormal investigators if I have over-simplified or misinterpreted this information in my novel.

Information on the unearthing of human remains is found at http://www.pc.gc.ca/eng/docs/r/pfa-fap/sec7/decouv_discov3.aspx and http://www.amick.ca/5-TheDiscoveryOfHumanRemains.pdf.

The Rural Mailbox Guidelines, of which Jake continually ran afoul, are found at https://www.canadapost.ca/cpo/mc/assets/pdf/personal/rmb_guidelines_e.pdf.

The nursery rhyme "The Well" is taken from http://www.apples4theteacher.com/mother-goose-nursery-rhymes/a-well.html.

And when Aunt Gertrude thanks Jake for taking the sadness from Jenny's eyes, you might have heard the echo of a line from Leonard Cohen's "Famous Blue Raincoat". Jenny's mom, Iris Campbell, would no doubt have approved.

About the Author

Lynn Clark was born in Woodstock, New Brunswick. She attended Acadia University in Wolfville, Nova Scotia, where she obtained a B.A. and an M.A. in English. She moved to Ontario in 1978 and now regards it as her home. She has worked variously as a proofreader and editor, technical trainer, program analyst, technical writer, project leader, and program manager. She retired in 2011 after working for almost thirty years with the federal government in Ottawa. Her husband of thirty-five years is the crime fiction novelist Michael J. McCann. They have one son, Timothy Daniel McCann.

CPSIA information can be obtained at www.ICGtesting.com
Printed in the USA
LVOW11s2324020116

468694LV00001B/1/P